FREEDOM

F-BOMB: SEALS LOVE CURVES, BOOK 1

MARY E THOMPSON

BluEyed Press

F-BOMB: SEALS LOVE CURVES

Welcome to the world of F-BOMB where a group of former SEALs have come together to protect the curvy women they love and the country they call home from the dangers of the world. They have the training and the knowledge, and they have the ability to kick some ass when needed. And it'll be needed.

F-BOMB: SEALs LOVE CURVES

Freedom

Fiancée (subscriber exclusive)

Forgotten

First

Failure

Friends

Family

Forbidden

Future

Finally

SUBSCRIBE NOW AT MARYETHOMPSON.COM

To being brave... whether than means kicking ass, trying something new, or just having confidence in yourself... you are brave

1

———

THE VIBRATING PHONE WOKE ARCHER FORD FROM A SOUND sleep. Well, as sound as his sleep ever was. He snatched it from the table next to his bed.

"What?"

A quick intake of breath on the other end of the line had the hairs on the back of his neck standing on end. He was on his feet, wide awake in seconds. Archer was ready for anything.

Or so he thought.

"Is this Archer?" the woman asked.

"Who is this?" he demanded. He never answered questions when he didn't know who was asking them.

"I need to know if I have the right number. Is this Archer Ford? Jaymes's brother?"

"How do you know my brother?" Archer asked, knowing he needed to get her talking if he was going to find out anything. He had a feeling in his gut, and his gut was never wrong. He just never expected the bad news to come from his brother.

"I'm his best friend. He told me to call you if I ever

needed something. And I... I need your help. Well, really, he does. And I didn't know who to call or what to do. I'm really worried. He never does this sort of thing. Maybe I'm overreacting, but—"

"Stop talking," Archer barked.

She shut up instantly.

"Now, tell me what the hell you're talking about. What's going on? Who doesn't do what sort of thing?"

"Jaymes. He disappeared a few days ago, and I don't know where he is. He hasn't been answering his phone, and he didn't tell me he was leaving, and—"

"Stop! My brother is missing?" Dread sank into Archer and hooked on to every nerve in his body.

"Well, missing is such a strong word. Maybe he's working on a project and his phone died."

"Has he ever done that before?"

She sucked in a breath. "Jaymes? No."

"He's never gone off without telling you?"

"No. Never."

"Are you fucking my brother?"

She gasped. "Who the hell do you think you are to ask me something like that? That's none of your business!"

"So, no," Archer said. But she wants to.

Lucky bastard. Archer couldn't remember the last woman who wanted him. And the voice on the other end of his phone was sultry and seductive and could get him hard in an instant if she weren't telling him his brother was missing.

Not kidnapped, she said.

He rolled his eyes.

"Fine, no. I'm not sleeping with Jaymes. What does that have to do with anything?"

"Because I need to know how much you matter to my

brother. If you're his girlfriend, whoever took him could come back for you to use as leverage. Where are you?"

"Do you really think they'd do that?" she whispered, her voice laced with fear.

Shit. Archer forgot he was talking to a civilian, not a fellow SEAL. Not that he could consider them his brothers any longer. He quit with the rest of them. He didn't want to go, but he wasn't given a choice like the others. Honorably discharged, they said. It meant the same fucking thing.

He was out. His career was over. There was nothing left for him.

"I don't know who 'they' are or what they're capable of, but anything is possible. If you're a friend and not his girlfriend, they might not care about you. If he really was kidnapped."

"His place was trashed. It looked like someone tossed it. That's the right word for it, right? When someone goes through looking for something?"

Archer nearly groaned. She was going to be a piece of work. "Yeah. Anyway. Stay where you are. I'll... be there in a few hours."

"What should I do if they come to get me?"

"Hide," Archer said, then hung up the phone.

He closed his eyes and took a deep breath. He had no desire to return home. He'd be happy if he never set foot in Western New York ever again. Hell, all of New York.

But he couldn't leave his brother. Especially when he had that feeling in his gut. Something wasn't right.

ARCHER PULLED into his brother's parking lot around five in the morning. He was exhausted from driving all night, but he was on high alert. He slid his Glock into the back of his waistband and headed for the door to his brother's building.

The door was locked, but easy enough to get into. He slipped inside and looked around. He'd never been in the building before, but it was like any other apartment building. Dark carpet, beige walls, dim lighting, and that never-ending smell of lemon-scented cleaner that only masked the deeper scent of multiple people living under the same roof.

He checked the numbers on the first floor. He'd never been to his brother's apartment, thought he never would be, so he had no idea which floor he lived on. Unit 17 couldn't be too high up, but Archer really had no clue.

Three floors up, he finally found it at the back of the building. He quickly picked the lock and let himself inside, closing the door with a soft click.

The apartment was dark. Blinds were drawn against the sunlight that would try to spill inside in less than two hours. Archer waited, listening, as his eyes adjusted to the space.

He was in a small entryway. A boot tray was on his left, and jackets hung on the wall behind the door. There was a small table in front of him and a tiny kitchen farther off to the left. He crept around the table and peeked into the kitchen. Nothing seemed particularly out of place. No dishes in the sink and only a few small appliances on the counter, but nothing that concerned him.

He continued into the living room, glancing around. His brother was always neat, putting his toys away and keeping his room spotless. He was the son their dad didn't have to get after about every little thing. Not like Archer. Jaymes was perfect, and Archer was a fuck-up. It was the story of their lives.

The living room was clear, so Archer kept going toward a

back hallway. He couldn't see around the corner, so he drew his gun. His hand shook. *Fuck.* He switched hands and shook it out. He closed his eyes for just a second, long enough to force his demons back into the grave where they belonged.

Archer swapped the gun to his right hand again and let it lead the way into the hall. A bathroom was right in front of him, and two bedrooms opened up a step farther into the darkness.

He took a step forward, going toward the bathroom, the easiest of the three to check, when he heard it. Nothing any normal person would pick up, but he wasn't normal. Hadn't been in far too long.

Breathing. Uneven. Fear or excitement? He didn't know.

Archer moved slowly, hoping he could catch the person off guard. He stopped his own breathing so he could just listen and pinpointed their position. In the first bedroom, the one directly across from the bathroom. Just inside the door. Probably either a gun or another weapon in hand if the person was waiting that close to the door.

He moved quickly once he knew where to go and stepped into the bedroom and pointed his gun right at the person's face.

A gasp. Then the shaky breath.

Definitely not someone threatening. Jaymes's girlfriend, maybe?

"Who are you and what are you doing here?"

"I'm Lily Scott," she whimpered. "I was just—"

"You're the one from the phone," Archer said, lowering his gun. "The best friend."

She sagged onto the bed, her whole body shaking. She drew her knees up to her chest and wrapped her arms around them and tried to suck in breath after breath.

Archer crouched down in front of her. The last thing he needed was her having a panic attack. "Breathe with me. Slow, deep breaths. Count to three. In, two, three. Out, two, three. In, two, three. Out, two, three."

To his surprise, she did what he said. She stared into his eyes and dragged in one ragged breath after another until there wasn't a hitch in each one.

"Feeling better?" he asked.

She nodded. "I think so. Um, who are you?"

His dark eyebrows shot up, and he almost laughed. She just sat there with him, after he pointed a gun in her face, and had no idea who he was? "You called me. I'm Archer."

Her eyes scanned him until the appraisal drove him to his feet. He didn't want to know what she saw when she looked at him. Especially not with the darkness that hung between them. In the harsh light of day, it would be a different story, but in the dark, Archer couldn't hide from the truth in the dark.

He smacked the switch and flooded the room with too much light. He let his eyes adjust for a second, then took a good look at the woman who asked for his help.

Jesus, she was beautiful.

She wore the tiniest pair of shorts he'd ever seen and a tank top that was so tight it might as well have been see-through. Not that he was complaining. Pink was definitely his new favorite color. Pink shorts, pink top, and pink nipples trying to peek out and say hi.

He was *up* to the task.

"I didn't think you could get here so fast. What time is it?"

"Five. You said my brother was missing. I thought this was his place, so I came here."

"It is," Lily said quickly.

Archer scanned the room, taking in the rumpled queen sized bed, the woman's clothes tossed around, and the mix of items that had to be his brother's and there was only one conclusion to draw. Lily might not be screwing his brother, but they were doing something.

"You live here, too?"

Lily shook her head. "No. I have my own place, but you said to stay put. I figured if Jaymes came home during the night, I could call you and let you know he was back. I didn't realize you were going to be here already."

Archer nodded and looked around. He didn't know his brother well. Not anymore. Once upon a time they were close, but that ended years ago, when Archer was ten and his brother was only six. It had been years since Archer had even seen Jaymes, let alone knew anything about his life. He was pretty sure Jaymes did something with computers, but what, he had no clue.

"Do you stay here often?" Archer asked for some unknown reason. It was obvious she was close to Jaymes, whether they were involved or not. She was at risk if Jaymes really was kidnapped. How often she spent the night was only relevant to the side of him that was trying to decide if he could sleep with her and not piss off his brother.

Lily shrugged, shifting her breasts and dragging his gaze back to them. They jiggled a bit when she moved. Even more when she talked. She liked to talk with her hands. Hell, she talked with her whole body. Her hips swayed gently as she spoke, and her hair, brown with blonde and red strung through it, curved around her breasts like lovers caressing her.

He was jealous of her damn hair.

"Are you even listening to me?" she asked, hands punching those sexy hips.

Archer shook his head. "Long drive."

Her irritation slid away, and genuine concern replaced it. "I'm sorry. I didn't even think about that. Can I make you some coffee? Or maybe you prefer tea. We have water and orange juice. Do you want breakfast?"

"Lily," Archer said loudly to get her attention. She'd already moved into the kitchen and flipped on every light in the apartment. Pans banged under a cabinet as she bent at the waist to retrieve them.

His brother was a damn saint if he wasn't sleeping with this woman.

"Eggs? How about an omelet? I make a killer omelet. Jaymes loves my... omelets." She turned watery eyes up to Archer. "Am I ever going to see him again?"

Archer couldn't think about that. Losing his brother wasn't an option. He'd lost too many of them during his time as a SEAL. He wasn't going to lose the only one he actually shared DNA with.

"You'll see him again," he promised Lily. "I'll find him."

She fell into his arms like she'd run out of energy to keep herself upright. Adrenaline was a bitch. One minute Lily was getting ready to make breakfast, and the next she was crashing in Archer's arms.

He held her awkwardly. It had been a while since he'd touched a woman, let alone had one in his arms. And the last time, she was definitely not crying. Screaming, panting, and moaning, yeah, but not crying.

She clung to him for a few seconds, long enough that his cock took notice of the curvy, warm woman in his arms. She smelled like every good thing the world had to offer. Like cookies and fresh air and woman all rolled into one. He wanted to press his face into her neck and inhale her deep, but he had no right. She belonged to Jaymes.

"I'm sorry," she said, taking a big step back. "I know you don't like people to lean on you. I just lost it. I've been so scared, you know. And I feel so much better with you here. Jaymes always said you could do anything, and I believe it. I know you'll find him and bring him back. And I really appreciate it."

Archer's mind spun with the load she dropped on him. Obviously, his brother talked about him. And it wasn't good.

The only problem was it was all true. He wasn't the kind of guy a person could lean on. He wasn't reliable. He always managed to fuck things up one way or another. He was there because he owed it to Jaymes. Archer had been trying to repay his brother for years, and this was his first opportunity. When he found him and returned him to his woman, Archer could crawl back in his hole and disappear again.

"Uh, yeah. I'll find him."

"Thank you," Lily said.

Her smile gutted him. She had faith in him. She trusted him. He didn't deserve either, but he'd do his best to deliver for her. A woman like her deserved to be happy. And if Jaymes made her happy, Archer would give up his own life to save him. It was the least he owed, to Jaymes and to Rodney.

"If I'm going to find him, I need some information from you. Tell me everything you know. About my brother, what he does, where he spends his time, everything. You're the only lead I have right now, so I need your help."

2

———

Lily couldn't stop talking. No matter how many times she told herself to just shut up, it didn't work. She always babbled when she was nervous, and finding your best friend's apartment trashed and knowing his neat-as-a-pin self would never leave even a dirty dish in the sink let alone trash his place, she freaked out.

But those nerves had nothing on the ones brought out by his sexy-as-all-hell brother.

Lily saw pictures of Archer before, but seeing a picture and being face-to-face with the man were two very different things. His skin was darker than Jaymes's was, like a golden honey that she was dying to dip her finger into for a taste. His eyes were the same dark chocolate color, bordering on black when she said something he didn't like. She really needed to get a handle on herself.

Archer topped her by at least eight inches, but at five-five, that wasn't something too unusual. What was unusual was feeling normal next to him. She had hips that threatened door frames, but she had nothing on his shoulders.

The thrill it set off in her sex was something she hadn't felt in far too long.

The best part was all the hardness of him that offset her soft parts. When she flung herself at him, she knew instantly it was a mistake, but she couldn't bring herself to let go until the solid strength of him seeped into her pores and gave her just a tiny bit of it. He was the kind of man who could stand in front of a firing squad and not blink. He had strength for everyone around him. It was what made him a hell of a SEAL, according to Jaymes, and exactly what she needed when she was terrified.

"Jaymes always tells me when he's doing something that's not normal," Lily explained. "We talk constantly. If he was off playing a new game or working on a project, he'd have warned me he'd be out of touch. He knows better than to run off without telling me where he's going."

Lily clamped her mouth shut and spun toward the stove. She busied herself pulling food out of the fridge to avoid explaining what she just admitted.

Without asking, Lily cracked half a dozen eggs into a pan. She chopped onions, peppers, and mushrooms and tossed them in when the eggs were almost done. She grabbed a bag of shredded cheddar and sprinkled some on top, then spun to give Archer breakfast.

He watched her as she moved. She could feel his eyes tracking her around the small kitchen. It was opposite hers on the second floor, but she spent enough time at Jaymes's that she knew her way around it just as well. Hell, she was the one who stocked his fridge most of the time.

"You spend a lot of time here," Archer said. It wasn't a question, more a statement he was figuring out. Learning her.

Lily nodded. "Yeah. Jaymes hates to cook so I do it. Cooking is a lot more fun when I have someone to do it for."

She sat across from him at the tiny table she insisted Jaymes buy when he moved in. It wasn't right to not have one, she told him. He wanted to put a bar in, but she wasn't having that. They weren't in college anymore. Thirty was way too old to have a bar instead of a dining room table.

Archer ate in silence, shoveling the food in so fast Lily wondered if he actually tasted any of it. She, on the other hand, was so anxious sitting in the same room as him that she could barely choke down the small amount of food she'd reserved for herself.

"Thank you for coming," she finally said, unable to take the quiet any longer. "I know Jaymes will be pissed when he finds out I called you, but I didn't know what else to do. I covered for him at work, but I don't know how long I can do that without making his boss suspicious."

"You know his boss?"

Lily nodded. "Jaymes has been there four years. I'm always his plus-one at company events and stuff. I've gotten to know all his coworkers pretty well. He's been looking for a new job for a while, but he doesn't really know what he wants to do. I told him I'd get him a job at the hospital, but he doesn't want to do that."

"Wouldn't that be a conflict of interest?" Archer asked, lifting his eyes to spear her with a look.

The venom in his eyes shocked her. She wasn't sure what he was after, but she wasn't feeling all that friendly toward him at that particular moment. His eyes were dark with a dangerous glint to them that rose the tiny hairs on her arms. She knew his job with the SEALs wasn't the friendly sort, but she didn't have any concept of how deadly the man in front of her could be until he set his glare on her.

"Why would it be a conflict of interest?" she asked, thanking God her voice was steady.

He quirked one dark eyebrow at her. The edge of his lips lifted, just enough to show that he found her question funny. "Nepotism and all that. Is it not frowned upon in your job?"

"Nepotism? That's for relatives. I'm not related." Realization dawned when amusement filled his gaze. "Really? Back to you thinking I'm sleeping with your brother? What do I need to do, slide under the table and give you a blow job to prove I'm not screwing my best friend?"

His expression turned murderous at her offhand comment, and she immediately regretted her words.

Was he the kind of guy who would take her up on that?

"That won't be necessary. I'm just trying to figure out why you're trying so hard to convince me you and my brother aren't together. You cook for him, you know his home, hell, you were sleeping in his bed," he waved his hand at her, "in that. Any sane person would draw the same conclusion I am."

Lily glanced down at her clothes and immediately crossed her arms over her chest. She was so terrified when she heard someone in the apartment she didn't think to grab her robe. Then when she saw who it was, and realized he wasn't there to kidnap or kill her, she couldn't think straight.

Jaymes was like a brother to her. She never thought twice about what she wore when he was around. He didn't look at her that way, so she dressed for comfort, even at night. Wearing something dowdy around Jaymes in the guise of modesty was wasted since he couldn't care either way.

"Excuse me," Lily said, pushing away from the table and

going to Jaymes's room. She had clothes in there, clothes she wore all day. Jaymes gave her a drawer in his room to keep stuff, but she felt guilty taking over his space so she kept a bag in the office. Which was where she found the pajamas.

She'd almost forgotten about them, but when she saw the silky fabric stuffed at the bottom of the bag, Lily couldn't resist wearing them.

Now she was regretting that decision. The weight she'd gained since she bought the silky pajamas turned them into laundry day pajamas over a year ago, and she'd added a few more pounds since then, making them nearly indecent.

She slipped on a pair of shorts that fell to her knees and snagged one of Jaymes's sweatshirts. She tugged a brush through her long hair and tied it up into a ponytail, then splashed cold water on her cheeks. Archer might be a pig, but she couldn't deny the way he lit her up.

Damn him.

She went back to the kitchen and was surprised to find him at the sink washing dishes.

"I was going to do that," she said.

He glanced over his shoulder and smiled. "You cooked. Nice sweatshirt."

"It's Jaymes's."

Archer turned off the water and dried his hands. When he turned, he leaned his hip against the edge of the counter and studied her. The darkness was gone, but she could sense the questions he wanted to ask.

She had a few of her own. Like why didn't he ever call his brother? Or visit? Or why didn't he cheer Jaymes on when he joined the Navy? They were virtual strangers, and it bothered Jaymes. Lily itched to lay into his brother and find out why they weren't closer.

"So, best friend, tell me what you know about my

brother disappearing," Archer said. Gone was the light she glimpsed for a second, and the opportunity to ask her own questions. He was in work mode, and she could tell nothing would drag him out of that.

ARCHER WATCHED Lily as she moved around. He was disappointed that she'd covered up, but it was for the best. The last thing he needed was to play in his brother's sandbox.

She rambled on about Jaymes's work and how much time he spent at the office. She worried about him not eating enough and his happiness. Archer didn't believe for a second that there wasn't more to the relationship between the two of them than friendship. She was either in love with Jaymes, or a mother hen. Archer never knew what either was like so he had no clue which was the truth.

Unless you counted Adrian Malone. Rocky to the rest of the Team, Adrian was as close to a mother hen as Archer had ever known. God knew his own mother couldn't have cared less.

"Okay, stop. What do Jaymes's eating habits have to do with his disappearance?" Archer asked Lily.

She sighed and threw her hands up. When they slapped against her thighs, her lip trembled.

Fuck.

Women in Archer's life cried for one of two reasons. Either they were trying to get him to do something he didn't want to do, or they were shot. A quick scan told him Lily didn't have any unapproved holes in her, which meant she was about to ask him to do something that would only piss him off.

"I don't know. I've never been through this. I'm freaking out, and you're sitting there so calm. He's *your* brother for fuck's sake, but I'm the one who's losing my damn mind. How are you so calm?"

She swiped the tears that slid off her lashes and crossed her arms again. He had to give her credit, she didn't act like she gave a shit if he was there or not. There was no request for him to hold her, or to make it all better, or even to go out and find Jaymes right then.

The fucked up truth of it was Archer would have done it if she'd asked. Most of the time when women cried, it made him ready to walk away that much faster. With Lily, he wanted to tuck her under his chin and take on every terrorist in the world to make her smile again.

"This is my job," he said, rising from his chair to stand in front of her. "I've spent the last twelve years of my life doing things you've never even dreamed of, finding people who were gone forever and bringing them back. I will find my brother."

She sucked in a breath, and her eyes went wide. "Do you think this is something the military is involved in? Has he been taken by ISIS or one of those terrorist groups?"

Jesus. That was why Archer hated the fucking media. The shit they spewed had sane Americans thinking the terrorist cells were down the street and waiting to nab unsuspecting people out of their homes. Yeah, the crazy fuckers wouldn't think twice about it, but they had bigger fish in mind than a computer geek from Niagara Falls.

"I'm sure the military has much more important things to do than chase down my brother."

Her face screwed up in an adorable scrunch that gave him a glimpse of the girl she was once. Questioning every-thing. Telling everyone around her what to do, no doubt.

"Okay, but don't you have to go? Some mission or something? Jaymes always talks about how busy you are and how little you're in the country. Honestly, I was surprised you answered your phone, and even more shocked when you showed up here. I know he's your brother and all, but—"

"I'm not in the Navy anymore," Archer said. He hadn't said the words aloud before. It gutted him to admit it, but it was the truth. She'd find out soon enough that he was sticking around, at least until Jaymes got back. Best to rip the band-aid off and spill now. "My unit was done and a bunch of guys decided to check out. I wasn't given a choice in the matter."

"Why?"

Archer slid a hand over his hair. Still military short since he'd only been out a week. If he was on base, he'd be looking for someone to cut it for him. But he wouldn't step foot on another one. He was out. Done. Retired, officially. Fired in reality.

They couldn't trust him any longer. It didn't matter that he didn't remember taking a shot at Rodney, there was no denying which direction the bullets that killed him came from. So Archer was out, Rodney was dead, and almost all the rest of them scattered throughout the country.

"It doesn't matter," Archer finally said. "Where's Jaymes's computer?"

Lily chewed on her lip and pointed toward the bedroom. Archer left her standing there, probably trying to figure out how she could get the hell away from him, and went down the hallway. The bedroom didn't show anything, but the other room was set up as an office. One computer sat front and center on a glass desk. Books lined a shelf behind the desk. A printer rested silently on the corner, cables neatly tied to the metal leg instead of dangling like most people would leave them. Archer was impressed that his brother cared that much about the appearance, but he was a computer guy. Liam "English" Johnson was the same way. The first thing he always did when they set up some place new was connect all his equipment and tie the cables together and out of the way. Seeing the precision in Jaymes's office surprised him. Few men outside the military were that careful.

Archer powered up the computer and searched through Jaymes's files. Lily didn't come in, but after an hour, Archer smelled something that made his stomach growl loudly. He pushed through, looking for something. He knew there had to be a clue somewhere, but he couldn't find it.

English would find it.

The thought made him pause. Liam was out. He bailed with the rest of them. Could he call him? It wasn't crossing any military boundaries. They were retired. They wouldn't be using the tools they had in the SEALs, just the skills. And if it meant finding his brother, it was worth the risk to Archer. He just hoped it was worth the risk to Liam.

Archer punched in the speed dial on his phone and waited for it to stop ringing.

"Johnson."

3

───────

Lily fiddled around in the kitchen. She hated feeling useless, but she wasn't much help to Archer. She heard him on the phone in the office as she pulled a batch of cupcakes out of the oven.

Busy work, Jaymes always said, but when he went to the store, he bought the supplies she needed. He stocked the things he knew she liked to eat, or bake, but rarely had anything for himself. Lily took care of that part and made sure Jaymes had plenty of snacks around.

She dried the mixing bowl and set it back under the stand mixer Jaymes only bought because she loved it. It would be awhile before the cupcakes were cool enough to frost, but Lily needed a sugar jolt to start her day. She was usually up early, but she was not a morning person, and being woken up by a guy breaking in to the apartment did little for her ability to function. Caffeine never helped, but sugar would.

Sugar, milk, butter, and vanilla went into the bowl. The rhythmic whirr of the blades lulled Lily. The kitchen was her happy place. She loved computers and running the systems for St. Nicholas Hospital, but cooking was her passion and her love.

Lily hummed to herself as she spun the ingredients into frosting. When it thickened and stuck to the edges, she turned the mixer off and lowered the bowl. She swiped her finger through the white paste and licked it, closing her eyes for a second to savor the sweet burst.

"Cupcakes?" Archer asked from behind her.

Lily jumped and spun, her finger still between her lips. She nipped the tip. Shaking it, she nodded. "I bake a lot. Is that okay?"

Archer shrugged. "They smell good."

Lily couldn't stop the rush of pleasure at the depth of his voice. His gaze flickered from her face to the bowl and then to her chest. Her nipples tightened under his appraisal, and she fought the urge to cross her arms. He couldn't see through her sweatshirt, although he'd gotten a hell of a look earlier.

"They're not really cool yet. If you eat fast, though, you can have one. I usually end up sticking them in the freezer so I can eat them faster."

Archer stared at her long enough that she grew uncomfortable. She turned back to the stove and grabbed the plate of cupcakes. She stabbed a knife into the frosting and slid it over the top of one of the cupcakes.

When it was done, Lily turned and handed the cupcake over to Archer. He raised one dark eyebrow and took the cupcake. His eyes locked on hers as he peeled back the baby blue wrapper and took a bite of the still warm cupcake.

He groaned as he chewed. His pink tongue darted out to capture a crumb that lingered on the edge of his mouth.

Lily licked her lips at the same time, imagining the taste on him. Her mouth watered at the thought. She had to turn away or she'd do something she regretted. Like find out what her cupcake tasted like on his lips.

She frosted her own warm cupcake and busied herself with eating it. Archer's was gone in three or four bites. She tried to be dainty about it, although she could have done the same. The last thing she needed to do was remind him that she had a few too many curves.

"Damn, that was good. Do you bake for a living?"

Lily snorted. "Um, no. I'm the Assistant IT Director for St. Nicholas Hospital."

Archer's brows winged up, but his eyes darkened. "You are?"

She nodded. "Yeah, why?"

"I called a buddy of mine. If Jaymes was taken, we think it had to do with his computer skills."

"Okay."

"If you're in the same field, you could be a target. Especially if they know both of you. Have you noticed anyone around?"

A chill raced up Lily's spine, and not a good one. It was terrifying enough that Jaymes was kidnapped, but the idea of someone watching her and coming after her made her feel violated.

Lily absently rubbed her arms and shook her head. "I haven't seen anyone. Do you really think someone's watching me?"

Archer shrugged. "There's no way to know. I would like to check out your place. If you're okay with that."

Lily nodded. "Yeah, of course. If it'll help Jaymes, I'll do anything."

She stuffed her feet into her sneakers and headed for the door. She grabbed her keys out of her purse and opened the door.

"Aren't you going to take your purse? Or anything else?"

"I live downstairs. I can come back up and get...it. Oh, um. You probably want the place to yourself now that you're here. Sorry. I wasn't thinking." She closed the door and moved to collect some of the things she had. "I'm so used to staying here, especially on the weekends, that I didn't think about leaving. I'm not trying to get in your way."

With heated cheeks, Lily grabbed her purse and one of the cupcakes and walked out. She could feel Archer following her, but he was silent as he moved. She stuffed the cupcake in her mouth to keep from blabbering that much more. She hurried down the flight of stairs until she came to her door.

Her hand shook as she tried to guide the key into the lock. Lily pulled back and shook her hand out. She took a deep breath and closed her eyes.

"Let me, Lily," Archer said, running his hand down her arm until he gripped her fingers.

She stepped to the side and let him open her door. He went inside first and stopped, putting his hand out.

"Lily, does your place always look like this?"

She peeked around him, and ice slid down her spine. She shook her head. "No. It doesn't."

"Stay here," he said, drawing a gun from his back. He moved into her place, disappearing around the corner toward her one bedroom. She stood, door open, watching where he went from the hallway.

It felt like hours passed before Archer reappeared again. His gun was gone, but there was tension in his shoulders that was new.

"No one's here. You need to go through all your stuff and find out if anything's missing."

Lily nodded and moved into her apartment. She felt

violated knowing someone had been in there. She wasn't the neatest person ever, but she definitely wasn't as messy as they left her apartment. She had no idea what someone would have been looking for, but it bothered her that they went through her stuff. Her stuff was personal.

She went to her room first. Archer stayed in the kitchen on his phone. Her clothes were everywhere, tossed on her bed and scattered all over the room. The thought of someone touching her panties, her clothes, her books... She shivered.

When she was done putting her room back together and couldn't find anything that was missing, she moved into the living room. Her computer was still in its normal spot. She turned in on and didn't notice anything that was off. She went through the rest of the room knowing Archer was watching her as he talked on his phone.

Lily was trying to figure out where she was going to spend the night when Archer hung up the phone. Maybe it was ridiculous, but she wasn't comfortable in her own home knowing someone was in there in the last twenty-four hours. She spent the night at Jaymes's place hoping she was being paranoid and he would be back, but with Archer there, she lost her safe harbor.

"Pack a bag," Archer said, moving into the living room and looking around. His gaze slid past her as she gaped at him.

"Excuse me?"

Archer finally turned the full brunt of his gaze on her. "You're not staying here, Lily. So either you pack a bag and come back up to Jaymes's apartment with me, or I'm bringing my stuff down here and sleeping on your couch. I'm going on the hunch you're not too big on sleeping here knowing someone was in here within the last..."

"Twenty-four hours," she said automatically, chewing on her lip.

"Twenty-four hours." Archer paused and caught her eye. "Your call, Lily, but I can't let you out of my sight until I know you're safe."

She finally nodded and went back to her room to pack a bag.

ARCHER BREATHED a sigh of relief when Lily walked away. He didn't want to have to force a woman he'd met a few hours ago to go with him. It wasn't his style, and it was, frankly, just a dick move. Even if it was for her safety.

The conversation he had with English was more than a little disturbing. Not just finding out that his brother's phone went dark three days ago, but learning that the same people were likely in Lily's apartment had him ready to tear up the whole fucking town to figure out what was going on.

Archer did his own search of the place while Lily packed. The mess had his fingers itching to clean it up. Twelve years of military service ingrained a need for everything to be neat and orderly in him. Seeing her items tossed around got to him, especially the colorful scraps of lace that were on her bed when he checked her room.

He adjusted his thickening cock at the image his mind conjured of her in just a pair of those. He really needed to get laid.

Lily's apartment was similar to Jaymes's except it was only a one bedroom instead of two. She still had the same small kitchen, but with a red mixer instead of the silver one upstairs. Her table was a bit more sturdy, and a lot more worn. Her couch was well broken in, but her laptop was new. Archer flipped it over and snapped a picture of the serial number and texted it to English.

Lily came back with a bag thrown over her shoulder and across her body, splitting the gap between her breasts and teasing Archer with the memory of what she looked like before he opened his damn mouth about her outfit. She could have stayed like that all day, but he had to call her out on her choice of sleepwear. Hell, he slept naked. What did that say about him?

Archer grabbed her laptop and took one of the bags in her hands, then swept the place one last time and followed Lily out the door.

As she was locking the door, one across the hall opened.

"Good morning, Lily," said a deep voice.

Archer glared at the man who only had eyes for Lily. He was almost as tall as Archer, but wiry by comparison. He wore glasses and smiled at Lily like she was grandma and he was the big, bad wolf.

"Hey, Blake."

"You going on a trip?"

Lily shook her head. Her lip trembled, and Archer had to step in.

"She's staying with me," he growled, sliding his arm around Lily's waist.

Blake looked over as though he really hadn't noticed Archer standing there. He extended a hand and smiled. "Blake Loren. Nice to meet you…"

"Archer Ford."

"Ford? Like Jaymes?" Blake asked with eyes that flipped between them.

Archer nodded. "Yep. Staying with my brother. Lil's going to stay up there with me, so I can have both my woman and my brother with me."

Blake didn't look as though he believed a word Archer was saying.

Archer had to sell it. If Blake was involved, he had to believe there was nothing strange about Archer being there, or about Lily leaving her place for a few days. If he wasn't involved, Archer just didn't need some random guy poking around.

He tugged Lily closer and pressed his nose to her hair. He inhaled deep, letting her cupcake and woman scent fill him. He hardened instantly.

Since he was already there, he took advantage of his position and gently suckled on her throat. She tasted as good as she smelled, making it hard for him to pull back.

Even harder when she moaned just loudly enough for him to hear.

"Yeah, okay," Blake said. "I, uh, I didn't realize you were seeing someone."

"It's new," Archer provided. "But I don't plan to let her get away."

Blake nodded. He turned to walk away, his shoulders slumping. He wasn't man enough to fight for Lily. Archer was a formidable opponent, but any man who couldn't see that Lily was the kind of woman you'd kick your best friend's ass for wasn't the man she needed.

Not that Archer was enough for her. He was damaged goods. It was risky saying they were together, but he didn't have a choice at that moment.

At least, that's what he told himself. It had nothing to do with his raging hard-on or how badly he wanted to stretch out over her and slide in home.

When the front door slapped closed behind Blake, Lily pushed away from Archer. "Why did you do that?"

"Who is he?" Archer demanded, ignoring her question.

"He lives across the hall. He has for over a year. Why are you acting like we're together?"

"Have you slept with him?"

Lily shot daggers at him. If looks could kill, he'd definitely be dead where he stood.

"I'm not like you, Archer. I don't sleep with every person I come into contact with."

"He seemed very interested in what you were doing," Archer said calmly.

"We talk. He's a nice guy. I've never slept with him. I'm not going to sleep with him. Just like I'm not going to sleep with Jaymes."

Archer held her gaze for a few more seconds. She didn't waver, leading him to believe she really was telling the truth.

"Good. Let's keep it that way."

Archer led the way up the stairs to Jaymes's apartment. Lily produced a key and let them back in. Archer did a quick sweep to make sure nothing had moved, then went back to the office.

He went through everything in Jaymes's office. English was searching his brother's computer, and Lily's. If there was anything to find on either computer, English would grab it. But Archer was better at getting his boots on the floor.

When he finished his search of the office, he moved to the bedroom. Nothing turned up suspicious, so Archer moved back into the living room.

"Are you hungry?" Lily asked from the kitchen. "Lunch is almost ready if you want to join me."

Archer nodded. His stomach rumbled loudly at the smells that spilled from the kitchen. It had been a long time since he had food cooked just for him. For years, he'd been eating in a cafeteria that served hundreds. Or digging out an MRE and pretending it wasn't as bad as it was.

Lily fixed him a plate of macaroni and cheese, broccoli, and a big piece of breaded chicken. He set his plate on the table and went back to the kitchen to find a drink. He poured two glasses of water and carried them to the table and sat down at the same time Lily did.

"Thank you for lunch," he said, meeting her eyes.

She nodded. "Comfort food. I hope you're okay with it."

Archer smiled. "You like to cook."

She nodded again, digging in to her food. "I do. I learned when I was pretty young and loved it. Jaymes says I'm a control freak because I like to be in charge of what we eat."

"It's a lot more than that, though," Archer guessed instinctively. He met her gaze and saw the admission there, even as he knew she wouldn't come out and tell him.

4

———————

Lily didn't like being called out. She didn't like other people knowing things about her that she didn't tell them. She couldn't help but wonder if Archer picked up on something or if he'd done a background check on her. Probably both.

"What makes you say that?" she hedged.

He shrugged. "Just a hunch. Single mom for most of your life. Married three times in just the last ten years, but probably more before that. I'm guessing you learned to cook because someone had to, and you liked it because it made you feel like there was one area of your life you were in control of. Still feel that way."

Tears welled up in her eyes. The food she was so excited to eat turned to sand on her tongue. Her stomach knotted and rejected what she already ate.

The cold, hard truth was she had no idea who Archer Ford was. Yeah, she knew he was Jaymes's brother. She'd seen enough pictures that she didn't doubt that. But from the moment they met, he had her off-kilter. He knew about her past, a past she'd barely told Jaymes about. Jaymes laughed with her when her mom got divorced and remarried. He knew the facts, but she never told him how hard it was when her dad left. She never told anyone, but Archer figured it out.

She pushed to her feet and glared down at him. "As much as I love having a complete stranger analyze me with information he got God knows how, I'm suddenly not hungry anymore."

Lily moved to put her plate in the sink, but Archer grabbed her wrist. She tried to tug it free, but he held on. "I apologize. I like to figure people out, and I'm having trouble figuring you out."

"So you keep insulting me to see what I'll react to? Congratulations. You finally found my weak spot. My mother treats me like I'm her best friend instead of her daughter. When you're thirteen, you don't need your mom giving you condoms and telling you to be careful, you need her to tell you not to have sex until you're older. When you're eighteen, you don't need her telling you you're on your own if you get pregnant now. Or trying to hire you an escort when you turn twenty-one, or asking you for money when you get your first real job. Then again, you're so good at your job you probably know about all of that, so I don't know why I'm even telling you."

She yanked her arm free and went into the kitchen. She rinsed her food down the drain and put her plate in the dishwasher. Without her own place to go, she couldn't get away from him. Yeah, she could leave, but whoever was out there scared her more than the man inside.

Which meant she was stuck.

ARCHER HATED WEAK WOMEN. Women who couldn't take care of themselves and leaned on the closest man to tell her how she should be feeling and what she should do.

Lily was not weak. She was pissed. She was hurt. She had a shitty past. But weak wasn't a word he'd use for the woman who stood toe to toe with him more than once over the last few hours.

He felt like dirt on the bottom of her shoe when she admitted what her mom did. The way she treated Lily. No one deserved to be tossed aside.

He struggled to say something to make her feel better because he was dirt on the bottom of a shoe. Not Lily's, but his father's. His father did the same thing as her mom, but opposite. Instead of treating him like a friend, he treated Archer like he wasn't even there. Nothing was the same after Jaymes got hurt. He'd hate to find out what his dad would say if Archer couldn't save Jaymes.

Good thing the bastard was dead.

Lily snapped off the water and dried her hands. She moved to go past Archer, but he blocked her way. "Lily."

She pulled in a breath, then looked up and met his eyes. The depth of her pain was something he knew all too well. Archer had the same ghosts in his eyes. The ones that never went away and followed you no matter where you were. A small house in Niagara Falls or a dessert in the Middle East or an apartment in the city that suddenly felt too small. It didn't matter. All that mattered was the voices of those ghosts reminding you of who you were.

"I did a background check on you," he confessed.

She scoffed and rolled her eyes. She took a step back and crossed her arms over her chest. She shook her head then glared up at him again.

"I had to know you were who you said you were. And I

needed to know you weren't involved in my brother's disappearance."

"Is any of this supposed to make me feel better?" she spat.

He nearly laughed. Caught himself just in time. Weak was not in Lily Scott's vocabulary. She was tough as nails. And she clearly had no trouble telling anyone who'd listen exactly what she thought.

"I didn't know any of that about your mom. I'm sorry you went through all that."

Her eyes shuttered before Archer even finished speaking. He felt her pulling away, but she didn't actually move.

"It was a long time ago. I'm good. If you'll excuse me…"

Archer sighed and moved from her path. She stepped around him, carefully not touching him. He thought about stopping her, but dropped his hand and let her pass.

Archer finished his lunch in silence, then went to check out Jaymes's truck. He wasn't sure he would know what his brother drove, but when he stepped outside, there were only two vehicles in the small parking lot aside from his, and he knew the red hybrid Civic wasn't Jaymes's.

The passenger door popped open with relative ease. Archer had all kinds of tricks up his sleeve, and getting into older cars was one of the many. The truck was spotless. Not even a straw wrapper stood out on the dark gray floor. Archer went through the truck, lifting mats and digging through the console and glove box. He checked under the seats and opened the bed of the truck, just in case there was something hiding back there.

He didn't find a damn thing. Nothing that could help him find his brother, or figure out who'd taken him or why. Archer felt helpless. He hated sitting around and doing nothing. He wanted to break something, or fuck someone, to get out all the aggression ripping through him. Sitting still wasn't helping Jaymes, but he couldn't tear through town and find him. He needed to be strategic, thoughtful, planned.

Nothing like his usual.

He always counted on his team to do the stuff that required brains. He was the brawn in any situation, and they were the brains. The ones who pointed his muscles in the right direction and told him to do his job.

He'd counted on his team for the last twelve years. Rodney was like his brother, more than his actual brother was. They'd gone through BUD/S together and were stationed together after that. He was going to be Rodney's best man, if he'd ever made it down the aisle. Instead, Archer was dodging phone calls from Monica. He couldn't tell her he was the reason she was a widow before she was a wife.

Archer slammed all the doors shut and swore. He thought for sure he'd find something that would lead him toward Jaymes. Who the hell could have taken him?

Archer had very little doubt someone had taken Jaymes. Even before he called English, Archer knew his brother was gone. The feeling in his gut was rarely wrong, and this one told him a shit storm was coming.

His finger itched to call his former CO, Brady Williams, or Daniel Dunn, his former XO. The two of them led their SEAL Team to countless flawless missions. Between the two of them, Archer was able to function after Rodney died.

He didn't deserve their kindness, but he appreciated the fuck out of it.

Archer let himself into the building and climbed the stairs to Jaymes's apartment. Every step of the way he tried to talk himself out of calling either Williams or Dunn.

Williams became like a father to him over the last few years, and Dunn was like an older brother. Someone who'd kick his ass when he needed it, but who was always there with advice and wisdom when required. After Rodney, Dunn was the person Archer was closest to.

Archer shoved his phone in his pocket and walked into the apartment. Lily wasn't in sight, but he could smell something cooking. The woman cooked constantly.

She peeked around the corner of the kitchen and gave him a tight smile. "I didn't know where you went."

"I thought I might find something in Jaymes's truck."

"Did you?" she asked hopefully, wiping her hands on a blue dish towel as she approached him.

Archer shook his head.

"I don't know if it's anything, but I got a message. I think it's from Jaymes."

"A message? When?"

"Twenty minutes ago. You weren't here." She pulled a phone from her back pocket and clicked a few things, then handed it over.

"Email?"

She nodded. "Read it."

Archer lifted the phone so he could read the message.

Dear Ms. Allendale,

Thank you for your interest in our services. Unfortunately, at this time, we don't have any openings that would suit you. We will keep your information for future reference, but please do not contact us again.

Sincerely,

Coco Dorchester

Archer raised narrowed eyes to Lily's smiling face. "I

have no idea what your rejection letter has to do with my brother missing."

Lily scowled and rolled her eyes. "It's not a rejection letter. I don't know anyone named Coco Dorchester, except your brother."

"Huh?"

"Have you ever seen those things that tell you your stripper name?"

Oh, fuck. Lily twisting around a pole in a tiny bikini and fuck-me-heels had Archer's cock pressing against the zipper of his pants.

He cleared his throat and hoped she didn't notice the wood he was sporting. "Okay?"

"Jaymes and I were talking about that last weekend. My stripper name, which is your first pet's name and the street you grew up on, would be Parker Allendale. His was—"

"Coco Dorchester," Archer supplied. His would have been the same. "Shit. So this is from Jaymes."

Lily nodded. "I think so. I don't know anyone else who would use those names. I almost deleted the email, but I figured I'd let you see it first, just in case."

Archer forwarded the email to his own email account and to English to analyze, then studied it again.

"What does this mean?" Lily asked quietly.

Archer pulled in a breath and shook his head. "I'm not sure. The good thing is it means he's alive."

Lily gasped. "Oh, God."

Archer was used to hostage situations that went wrong. Many did, especially when dealing with terrorists who didn't care who they killed. For them, it was a sport to kill someone. They'd take a person of interest, make demands, and kill the hostage anyway. Just to prove they could.

Archer tried to remind himself he was dealing with

people instead of ruthless terrorists, but it was hard to break that habit. He was a kill first, ask questions later kind of guy. And these sons of bitches were holding his brother hostage.

His phone rang, and Archer knew without looking it was English. He handed Lily her phone back and grabbed his. "Go."

"There aren't any indicators where it came from, but if she says it's Jaymes, I'm not going to argue. It looks like it bounced around the world a few times to scramble the original spot. One thing is clear, Ford..."

"I know," Archer confirmed. "Stay away."

He met Lily's gaze as he said the words, knowing she would understand. Tears welled up in her eyes. He wanted to comfort her, but he knew better than to get involved with a woman like her. Archer was a fuck 'em and forget 'em kind of guy. Everyone who got too close to him got hurt. It was better for Lily if he kept his distance. Just being in Jaymes's apartment with her put her at risk, but he couldn't leave her alone. Not when he knew whoever took Jaymes searched her place also.

Lily turned back to the stove, and Archer focused on what English was saying.

"There's something at the bottom, in the disclaimer, that could point in the right direction. I don't know if it's anything, but I'm looking into it. It looks like an automated message added by something in the system."

"That could tell us where the original message came from."

"Yeah, but it could also be something to make us chase our tail. They had to know Jaymes would try to contact someone. I wish I had the resources we had on the Team."

Archer nodded and rubbed the back of his neck. "I agree. I was thinking about that earlier. I'm not normally the brains, but I'm the only one here. It's fucking impossible to think straight right now."

His gaze drifted to Lily's creamy legs, on full display for him. Her cotton covered ass tempted him as she bent over to slide a pan of something into the oven. He nearly groaned when she tossed her head and flipped her hair over her shoulder, giving him a peek at her bare neck.

He could definitely get lost in her for a while.

"We'll find him."

Archer nodded, his mind going back to his missing brother instead of the beautiful woman who teased him without even knowing she was. "I hope so."

English promised to let him know if he figured out anything else, then they hung up. Archer pulled up the email on his phone. He read it again, looking at the disclaimer in more detail. There wasn't anything that stood out to him, but he didn't know his brother as well as he should. It had been a long time since Archer and Jaymes were close. Since Archer thought he had a right to know his brother.

Luckily for him, he had a Jaymes expert in the kitchen, cooking dinner for him. Twenty-four hours earlier, he didn't even know Lily existed. Now, his brother's life depended on her. On her being able to pull minuscule clues from an email Jaymes probably risked his life to send. A warning.

Jaymes was protecting Lily. It was clear how much he cared about her, and how she felt about him. Archer owed his brother a lot, but keeping his hands off the woman his brother might have a thing for was the least he could do while he tried to save his life.

Archer just wasn't sure if that was a mission he would be successful at.

5

LILY FINALLY TOOK A DEEP BREATH WHEN ARCHER LEFT THE
kitchen. When she walked out earlier to show him the email
and found the apartment empty, she had a minor panic
attack. She was convinced for a few seconds that someone
had taken Archer right out from under her nose.

Then she ran to the door and saw him bent over
searching Jaymes's truck and she felt better. Hotter, but
better.

The man could fill out a pair of jeans like no one she'd
ever seen.

Cooking dinner kept her mind off how attracted to him
she was. It wasn't like her to get so hot and bothered over a
guy. She preferred her men the same way she liked her
chocolate. Momentary pleasure, with lots of variety.

Not that she'd sampled much of the male variety lately.
Casual sex had lost some of its appeal, and she was *not* interested in a relationship. Relationships were overrated.

She knew enough about Archer to know he didn't do
relationships any more than she did. As a career SEAL, he
probably didn't have time to commit to anyone, but Jaymes

implied it was more than that. He said Archer had never had many relationships at all. As brothers, they barely had one, so Lily wasn't surprised by that admission.

It was one of the few things the brothers had in common. Jaymes dated infrequently, but he and his brother seemed to be polar opposites in every other way. Where Jaymes was all brains, Archer was clearly the brawn. Jaymes was emotional and flew off the handle when he got frustrated, but Archer seemed to be in complete control of every aspect of himself. She could always read when Jaymes was frustrated, but Archer looked like he was ready for the beach at any given time with his laid back, almost vacant expression.

Lily's sex tingled at the thought of taking Archer to a beach. It was likely the only way she'd get to see him in something other than his jeans and black t-shirt. Not that she was complaining about those, but she wouldn't mind spending a few hours tracing the fine lines of his muscles with her eyes.

Or her fingers.

Or her tongue.

Damn. Her thighs arched with the effort to clamp them closed. Those muscles didn't get much exercise. She wasn't one of those women who exercised so she could eat whatever she wanted. She was one who ate whatever she wanted and said she really should take up exercising one day.

Jaymes constantly tried to get her to go with him to the gym, but despite the membership she paid for, she'd only stepped foot inside a handful of times. She could think of plenty of things she'd rather be doing than going to the gym.

At the moment, Archer topped that list.

Lily groaned at herself and closed her eyes. That didn't do anything except play her fantasy of dressing up in a chef's coat and hat, leaving the buttons open down the front, and having a sexy guy make use of everything in the kitchen in ways she could only imagine.

Of course, the guy took the shape of Archer, giving a whole new level of hotness to her fantasy. Not that she'd ever act it out.

Lily opened her eyes and pulled in a deep breath. Getting lost in the guy who was there to save her best friend was the worst kind of stupid. Talk about hero worship. She knew better. She'd seen her mom fall for one too many guys after they'd saved her from one disaster after another. It never worked, and Lily knew enough not to think it ever would.

"Do you always cook like this?" Archer asked, walking back into the kitchen.

Lily nodded. "I try to. I like to cook. Jaymes likes to eat. It works for both of us."

"What are we having? Assuming you're willing to share."

She smiled at him and noted how much more attractive he was with a teasing glint in his eyes. As if he needed to be more attractive. "Garlic parmesan chicken with green beans and corn casserole."

Archer nodded. "Sounds good. Can I help with anything?"

Lily wasn't sure what to make of his offer, but she enjoyed cooking with other people. Jaymes usually sat in his office while she cooked. Once in a while, her friend, Stephanie, would cook with her, but she hadn't seen Stephanie in a few weeks.

"I'm just working on the green beans now. Everything else is in the oven."

"How about I open a bottle of wine? Or do you prefer beer?"

Lily shook her head. "I drink it all."

Archer barked a laugh that drew Lily's attention. She smiled in return and felt normal for the first time all day.

"I'm grabbing a beer. It looks like Jaymes drinks the same kind I do."

"Actually," Lily said, "those are mine. Jaymes prefers wine or whiskey."

Archer shook his head. "I feel like I should have known that." He was quiet for a few minutes. When he spoke again, he asked, "How much has Jaymes told you about me?"

Lily peeked back at him over her shoulder. "I don't know. As much as any guy would talk about his brother. He thinks you're great, and he regrets that you two aren't closer. He wanted to be like you, you know? He adores you, although he'd kill me if he found out I admitted that to you. He said you were always more than a big brother to him, you were like an idol. Someone he could watch but not touch. Someone who was there, but wasn't there. It bothered him when you left, but he got it. He would have gone after you if your parents weren't so adamant that he go to college. He followed you after that, but—"

"Followed me? What are you talking about?"

Lily clamped her mouth shut. Rambling had gotten her into more trouble than it'd gotten her out of. She did not need to tell Archer just how much Jaymes idolized him. To the point of trying to become a SEAL, and failing. He never wanted Archer to know that part. He promised her he'd tell his brother he was a SEAL after he made it. When he rang out two weeks in, he felt like an even bigger failure and swore her to secrecy.

Secrecy she'd kept all of twelve hours after meeting the one person Jaymes never wanted to tell.

"He, um, he moved to California after college. He said you went there, and he wanted to be closer to you."

Archer held her gaze for a beat too long, but Lily kept her lips closed up tight. Just as she was about to fold, he said, "I never knew that. But I'm realizing there's a lot about my brother I never knew."

Lily breathed a sigh of relief and removed the green beans from the heat. She turned off the oven and pulled out the chicken and corn casserole. Everything smelled good enough to make her stomach rumble loudly.

"Guess I'm not the only one who's hungry," Archer said.

Lily slapped her palm over her belly and nodded. "Yeah, sorry."

Archer shook his head. "Nothing to apologize for. I love a woman who enjoys her food."

Lily snorted. "I enjoy food a little too much."

Archer's gaze slid down her figure, lighting sparks up all over her skin. She'd traded Jaymes's sweatshirt for a pair of cotton shorts and a comfortable top when she got out of the shower, but he looked at her like she was wearing lingerie. And looked good in it.

"From where I'm standing, and the view I got this morning, there isn't too much of anything on you."

Lily's thighs clenched at the heavy, lust-filled tone of his deep voice. It skittered down her spine and settled in her sex. She should have grabbed one of her vibrators when she packed a bag to stay with him for a few days. The man was a walking orgasm waiting to happen.

Lily smiled faintly at him and ducked her head. She didn't do compliments. She could dish them out without a second thought, and she meant them, but accepting them was almost impossible.

"I don't say things I don't mean, Lily. You're a beautiful woman."

"Thank you," she whispered. Her cheeks heated at the sincerity in his tone. She focused on filling two plates with food and brought them to the table.

"Thank you for cooking. Again. This looks great. I haven't had a lot of home cooked food."

"How long have you been out of the Navy?"

"A month," Archer answered.

Lily's eyebrows shot up. "Wow. Jaymes didn't mention it."

Archer shook his head. "That's because he didn't know."

"Oh."

Silence filled the space between them as they both ate. Lily wanted to ask Archer why he kept his distance from Jaymes, why he never called his brother, why the two of them seemed little more than strangers.

But she kept silent.

"Did Jaymes ever tell you he broke his arm when we were kids?"

Lily looked up in shock and nodded. Jaymes complained about his arm being sore if he didn't take a break once in a while or if he slept on it wrong. All she knew was that he broke it, but Archer made it sound like there was more to the story.

"Did he tell you what happened?"

"Um, no. It bothers him sometimes, but he's never said much about it. He was pretty young, I thought."

Archer nodded and pushed away his empty plate. "He was six. Our mom was at the grocery store, and Dad was in the garage working on something. I don't remember. A car or building something. It doesn't matter. Anyway, we were playing soccer. Jaymes just started playing, but I'd been playing for a while. He was good. I thought I was better."

Archer paused, giving Lily a chance to appraise him. He looked tortured, which made her want to comfort him. A funny thought for a guy who she assumed never needed another person his whole life.

"Jaymes beat me. He... I got mad. I didn't think my little brother should be able to score a goal on me, so I was pissed off. I was angry and shoved him. He landed wrong on his arm, and it broke."

"You were a kid," Lily argued.

"I was stupid. I was bigger than him. Stronger. He was only six. I never should have done what I did. Our dad blamed me, which he should have. Every day I've regretted what I did. I've kept my distance from Jaymes because of it."

Lily wanted to reach for him, but she knew it wasn't her place. He looked so tortured, like it really had eaten at him for years that he hurt his brother when they were young. Jaymes never admitted what happened, even through school when other people would pick on him in class. The favorite joke was that Jaymes couldn't get a date and the only way he got laid was with himself. They were ruthless when his arm would bother him, but Jaymes never once said his brother broke his arm. As far as he was concerned, Archer was perfect.

"He never blamed you. I hope you know that. Obviously you blame yourself, but he never did."

Archer laughed mirthlessly. "He should have. I've done a lot of stupid shit in my life. Jaymes was just the first of many victims who got too close to me."

Archer pushed away from the table and walked away. A door closed a few seconds later, shutting Lily out of his world.

"Just as well," she told herself.

ARCHER'S PHONE rang just as he closed the door to the office. He felt more lost than he had in years. He had a purpose, a mission, a goal for his life. Every day was scripted by someone who knew what the bigger picture looked like.

And he was lost in a sea of nothingness that had him going slowly insane.

"Ford," he answered the phone.

"Why the fuck didn't you call me?"

Archer couldn't help the smile that curled his lips, even if he didn't appreciate the tone of the voice. "Mr. President."

"Cut the shit. Why didn't you call me?"

Archer sighed and ran a hand over his hair. Daniel Dunn was Archer's XO and would have been a CO if he hadn't turned in his papers with the rest of them. Too much shit went down during their last tour, and they were all done. Archer never thought Dunn would leave, but he said he couldn't handle the same shit every day without knowing what he was fighting for anymore.

Dunn could talk any of them into anything with a smile. He earned his nickname for his skills in diplomacy and coercion. He would have been a great president if he ever had the interest. "We're free men. That means I shouldn't be bugging you with this shit."

"But you can bug English? Fuck you, dude. I'm on my way. So's everyone else."

"No, you guys don't need to come."

"Too late. You don't get to vote on this one. Shit hits the fan, we have your back. Get some sleep. We'll be there early."

Archer stared at the phone for a full minute before the

conversation registered. He didn't deserve their kindness, but for his brother, he'd take all the help he could get.

He had his hand on the door to tell Lily his team was coming when he remembered his confession to her. He was lucky she didn't throw him out on his ass. She had every right to. Jaymes would be less than thrilled to see him, and any best friend of his likely knew it.

He didn't know what possessed him to tell her about breaking Jaymes's arm. He'd never told anyone, even Rodney. Before that day, he thought of his brother as his best friend. After that day, Archer stayed away. When Jaymes got his cast off, he wanted to play with Archer, but the glare he got from their father had Archer sulking off to his room instead of going outside with his brother. It wasn't long before Archer had better things to do than play with his little brother. Girls and sports and friends became more important than anything else when he was in high school. Then he enlisted and disappeared, only returning when he had to. Joining the SEALs was a great way to ensure he had a ready excuse at all times.

Jaymes went on with his life, and Archer disappeared into his. They were never close again, like Archer wanted. That was the only reason he'd driven from DC to Niagara Falls when Lily called. He knew he wasn't to blame for Jaymes's disappearance.

Archer killed time in the office, checking his email and making sure all his bills were paid. He admitted to himself he was stalling before he had to tell Lily they were expecting company, but it didn't change the fact that he was.

When he heard her in the bathroom, Archer finally convinced himself he couldn't delay any longer. It had been a long day, and they were both exhausted. Without anywhere else to go, they had to find a way to share Jaymes's apartment.

With only one bed.

Archer's cock rose at the thought of sharing the bed with Lily. He could make good use of a soft, horizontal surface with her buried beneath him. It would do his psyche a helluva lot of good to have her scream for him all night. Especially since he knew his team wasn't showing up empty handed in the morning. They were going to have equipment Archer couldn't begin to figure out how to find. They'd jump head-first into finding Jaymes. It was why they were coming, but Archer knew it would put a serious block in his way.

No. It was for the best. Lily deserved more than he had to offer a woman. She was a forever type, and he knew better than to fuck with women like her.

The bathroom door opened, and she stepped out. Archer watched her for a few seconds before she realized he was there and jumped.

"I didn't mean to scare you."

She shook her head. "It's fine. I wasn't expecting you."

She was wearing those tiny little pajamas again. Her nipples pressed against the thin fabric, teasing him. His eyes were glued to her chest with no help of removing them. It wasn't like he'd never seen a beautiful woman before, but it had been far too long since he'd seen one who made him forget his own name.

"Archer?"

Yeah, that was it.

"Hmm?"

"Are you okay?"

His eyes snapped to hers. He should be embarrassed that he was staring at her, but he couldn't muster it up. She was beautiful, and he was hard just looking at her. Hell, he was hard just thinking about her.

He wasn't sure he could keep his hands to himself.

6

"Archer?" Lily squeaked again. The way he looked at her had her thighs throbbing. It wouldn't take much for her to come. Not when she was already soaked and aching.

"Go to bed, Lily," he said roughly.

"Why?"

"Because I'm bad for you. I'm bad for everyone. And you're too good and sweet to be messed up with someone like me. My team is coming in the morning. You need some rest."

The speed with which he changed subjects astounded her. One minute he sounded like he wanted her, and the next he was talking about a team.

"What team? What are you talking about?"

"My Team. The SEALs I worked with."

"They're coming here?"

Archer nodded.

"How many people?" Lily was getting more than a little anxious. They were in a two bedroom apartment that only had one bed. She didn't mind sleeping on the couch, or the floor, but it was hard to accept that she'd be lucky to get a chance to take a decent shower when her own apartment was just downstairs.

"Six or seven. I'm not sure who's coming."

"Where are we going to put them all? We can't fit that many people in here."

"We'll figure that out tomorrow. It'll be good for everyone to be together, but the lack of beds will be a problem."

"Some people can stay in my apartment if you think it's safe."

"It's not safe for you to be there alone."

She looked up at him. "If you were there it would be fine. Whoever was there probably knew I was up here. They know who I am and where I am."

Archer rubbed his chin and nodded. "True. We'll figure it out tomorrow. Get some sleep."

Lily nodded. "I'm going to grab my stuff and I'll get out of your way."

"You're sleeping in the bedroom."

Lily shook her head. "No. The couch is too small for you to sleep on. You take the bed."

"Lily, I'm not arguing about this with you. You're sleeping in the bed. I'll take the couch. If someone breaks in, I can't protect you if you're out there alone."

Her breath rushed out of her in a whoosh, leaving plenty of room for fear. "You think someone's going to come here?"

Archer shook his head. "I doubt it, but I'm not willing to take that chance. I'm going to protect you."

"Even from you?"

His eyes darkened. He sucked in a ragged breath, his chest lifting. He still wore the jeans and black t-shirt he had on when he scared her awake at gunpoint. It seemed like she'd known him much longer than sixteen hours.

"Especially from me. Lock your door, Lily."

He pushed her gently into the bedroom. She stood on the other side of the threshold, staring him down, until he pulled the door closed between them.

"Lock it, Lily."

She smiled and flipped the lock.

"Good night, Lily."

"Night, Archer," she said to the door.

Lily waited until she heard the bathroom door close, then moved away from the door. She had no excuse for leaving the room, but she had an urge to push him. She felt safer knowing Archer would be in the living room all night, and that he'd protect her if anyone tried to get in.

Lily never had a guy in her life who watched out for her. Jaymes was there for her, but she still felt alone most of the time. Her father took off when she was young, and she never had any brothers. The men her mom dated, and married, were all duplicates of her worthless father. She was more or less on her own.

She could take care of herself. She always had. But there was no match for a badass SEAL who could kill someone with his bare hands if he needed to.

It didn't hurt that he had her heating up like an oven on high.

Lily slid into bed but was restless. She could hear Archer moving around the apartment. It was almost impossible to ignore his footsteps, especially when they paused outside the bedroom door for a bit too long.

Lily tossed and turned until she finally gave up. She needed a release, and without one of her trusty vibrators, her fingers were going to have to do the trick. She closed her eyes and pictured Archer and within seconds she was ready to fly. She tried to stifle her moans and whimpers, but she wasn't sure she did a very good job.

She came hard and fast, like she normally did when she was alone. It was really depressing that her sex life had been relegated to masturbating in her best friend's bed while she imagined his brother's fingers between her thighs, but that was her life.

At least she could sleep after that.

ARCHER NEARLY BROKE the door down when he heard Lily whimper. First he thought she was crying, but the needy tone told him a very different story. He stayed there until she breathed through her climax, then locked himself in the bathroom and replayed those sexy sounds until he was the one coming.

He stripped off his shirt and jeans and collapsed on the couch with a blanket over his waist. The pillows left a lot to be desired, but it was nowhere near the worst sleeping conditions Archer had ever been in.

He passed out quickly, but his dreams tangled his mind until Rodney and Lily were front and center. He couldn't remember anything when he woke up, but he knew he'd dreamed about them all night.

It was still dark out when Archer got up. After years on the other side of the world, his internal clock was FUBAR. He'd been told it would take some time, but he hated that answer. It was like telling an alcoholic one drink wouldn't kill them. Wrong fucking thing to say.

Archer took a quick shower and got dressed in a clean pair of jeans and another black t-shirt. It was easy to pack when everything he wore was the same thing. Even easier to get dressed.

When he opened the bathroom door, the bedroom door was already open. He listened carefully until he picked up on faint sounds coming from the kitchen.

"Sorry I woke you," he told Lily after he stashed his dirty clothes and shampoo back in his bag.

"You didn't," she said. "I'm usually up early."

"This early?"

Lily looked at the clock and nodded. Just after six.

"I don't know many people who like to get up this early."

She shrugged. "I didn't say I liked it, just that it's normal for me. It's a pain when my friends want to go out, but I haven't been able to sleep past seven ever."

"Yeah, me neither."

They were both silent for a few moments. Archer peeked over her shoulder to see what she had on the stove and was surprised when it was French toast.

"Are you hungry?" Lily asked, handing over a plate loaded with thick slices.

"Always. Thanks. I was going to cook."

"I like cooking. Plus, it keeps my mind off all this."

Archer nodded. He understood the thought. He hated to think of what happened to his brother. No clues, no demands, no ransom. It had been days. Five days. It fucking gutted Archer to start thinking of the search as a recovery instead of a rescue, but that was likely what it would be.

"What time will your team be here?" Lily asked.

Archer glanced at his watch. "Dunn said early, so within an hour I'd guess."

She turned and glanced at him over her shoulder. "Wow. That is early. I'll make sure there's enough food."

"You don't have to."

"It's the least I can do. I feel like every day that passes reduces the chance that Jaymes is coming back. I should have called you earlier. Maybe he'd be okay."

Her voice trembled. She sucked in a breath, but her shoulders shook.

Dammit.

Archer couldn't let her stand there and cry. He was up out of his seat and pulling her into his arms before he could convince himself it was a really bad idea.

Lily let him hold her, burrowing into him just like she did the day before. She tucked her head under his chin and held tightly to him for a long few minutes.

Archer's dick rose as he held her. She was wearing the same tiny pajamas she wore the day before, and his body noticed even before she was in his arms. There was no way she missed his erection, but Archer wasn't going to draw any attention to it. He just held her, stroking up and down her back and breathing in the comforting scent of her fruity shampoo.

She lifted her head from his chest and lifted endless blue eyes to his. She tilted her head and lifted onto her toes, her lips drawing closer to his with each breath.

"I'm not so sure this is a good idea," Archer said weakly.

"I'm not known for my good ideas."

She meant for him to smile, but his lips turned down. He didn't want to think about all the other men she'd been with. He wanted to erase them all in her mind until the only one she would ever think about was him.

"Lily. This isn't real. You don't want me."

"How do you know what I want?" she asked, her voice soft and teasing.

The early morning messed with his head. Archer was never himself so early. Too many bad decisions were made due to lack of sleep, and he wasn't going to let Lily be one of them. "Because I'm not good enough for you."

"I think I should be the judge of that."

He wanted to let her decide, but she'd regret it. She'd find out exactly who he was and wish she'd never gotten involved with him.

"Lily," he groaned, his resolve weakening as she pressed her curvy body against him. His cock throbbed, ready to get in on the action she was goading him into.

She blinked up at him, innocent eyes turning him inside out. Jesus. He needed to get laid if one woman could affect him this much. He speared a hand into her hair and was a breath away from claiming her lips when someone pounded on the door.

Archer glanced toward the couch where he left his gun and tucked Lily behind him, all thoughts of getting her naked taking a backseat to protecting her.

She vibrated against his back and whispered, "No one should be able to get into the building without a key."

The person pounded on the door again, then called out, "It's me."

Archer sighed and turned to Lily, squeezing her arm. "It's my team."

She nodded, still shaking.

"You're safe, Lil. I'm not going to let anything happen to you."

She nodded again.

"Go get some clothes on, sweetheart. I'll let them in."

She nodded and finally turned toward the bedroom.

Archer waited until she was out of sight, then went to the door. He opened it with a grin. Dunn was on his knees, tools stuck in the doorknob.

"I always knew you had a thing for me," Archer joked, grabbing his cock and wagging it toward Dunn.

Dunn rolled his eyes and rose to his feet. He tugged the pins from the lock and grabbed Archer for a rough one-armed hug. "You wish you could get someone as good looking as me to suck your dick."

Archer laughed and stepped back for his former-XO to walk inside. Right behind him was Liam "English" Johnson with his computer, then Jack "Squirrel" Farrell, and Ryker "Dex" Hamilton. Archer slapped backs and traded insults as the guys muscled their way into his brother's apartment.

"Slade and Adrian are on their way. And I talked to Williams."

Archer couldn't believe all of them were there, or on the way. He owed every guy in the room his life, and they'd say they owed him the same. They'd become brothers over the years, all of them closer than any family Archer had ever known. That was what happened when you spent every waking moment with the same people, suffering through the worst of hell and coming out the other side.

"Thanks." Archer took a second to swallow the cotton in his throat. "Means a lot."

"All good if you cooked for us. Something smells good, and it sure isn't your rank ass," Jack said, moving toward the kitchen. "Oh, even better. Good morning."

Archer turned in time to see Lily's cheeks flush and Jack grab her hand and kiss the back of it.

"Hello."

"Are you here with Archer?" Jack asked.

Lily shook her head. "I'm Lily. I'm the one who called him. Jaymes is my best friend."

Jack dropped her hand and took a step back. "Damn. And here I was getting my hopes up that you were single."

Lily's eye roll was apparent from across the room. "I am single. I don't know why no one believes that when I say Jaymes is my best friend."

Four sets of eyes swung toward Archer, pinning him in place. Lily's followed after a second, but there was a light in hers. And a challenge.

"She said they're not sleeping together."

Jack edged closer to Lily again. "Then I guess you're free game, huh? I saw her first," he threw over his shoulder to the others.

"Like hell," Archer blurted. "I've been here since yesterday."

Jack's lips curled into a grin, and he took a step back again. He looked like a fucking dancer in front of Lily, trying to get her to join him. "Excuse me, sir. I guess she is spoken for."

Archer didn't respond. Lily wasn't his, but seeing one of his friends hit on her had him ready to dig his gun out of his bag and challenge Jack. Bad move since the guy was a fucking sniper, but Archer would take a bullet for Lily. He knew that without even thinking about it.

"Um, I made breakfast," Lily said, her voice a little shaky. "If you guys are hungry. Archer said you'd be here early."

The guys dug in to Lily's breakfast, destroying every slice of French toast she set out. Archer made his way over to her and asked if she ate.

"Yeah, I grabbed some while you guys were talking."

"Good."

"Why didn't you correct them?"

"About what?" he asked, unable to meet her eyes.

"Really? Is that how you're going to play it? I didn't figure you for a chicken."

Archer snickered and turned to look at her. "Fine. I

didn't correct them because when they pounded on the door, my dick was hard and pressed against you. Because you might not be mine, but I'd be lying if I said listening to you make yourself come last night didn't make me want you. I'm no good for you, but I'm not going to stand here and watch one of these fuckers talk you into their bed."

Lily snorted. "Aren't they your friends?"

"Absolutely. I'd give my life for any of them. That doesn't mean I want them touching you."

Lily smiled. "Good to know."

7

———

LILY HAD TO ADMIT SEEING ARCHER JEALOUS WAS A BOOST TO her confidence. She didn't normally think twice about guys who got jealous, but Archer was even hotter when he went all alpha on her.

Which just meant she had to get him to do it again.

"How's breakfast guys?"

Jack slid out of his seat and dropped to one knee in front of her. "Forget about Archer and marry me, Lily. I'll protect you, and I have a bigger dick than he does."

"You wish," Archer said from behind her.

Jack shook his head. "He's lying to protect himself. He doesn't like the beautiful ladies knowing he has a tiny cock. It makes it harder for him to pick them up."

Lily laughed at them. If Jack thought Archer was tiny, she was afraid to know how big he was. The thick rod that was pressed against her stomach before the guys showed up was more than big enough for her.

Archer growled and moved closer to Lily. His heat radiated against her spine, warming her up. A large palm slid around her waist and tugged her back against him. His fingers edged under the sweatshirt she threw on when the guys knocked on the door.

It was bad enough Archer saw her in the tiny pajamas she wore. She wasn't showing off everything she had to the whole team.

"Back off, Squirrel."

Jack scowled at Archer and snapped his mouth shut. The other guys hooted with laughter. Lily turned to face Archer and asked what was so funny.

"City boy here didn't like doing PT without food, so he started hiding bags of nuts in his pocket before he'd go out. The bag broke one day, and he had a posse of squirrels chasing him down."

Lily tried not to laugh, but it was just too funny to think about a big guy like Jack being followed by squirrels. She could see him being gentle with the creatures, but she didn't imagine anyone wanted to be chased by a pack of squirrels.

"Screw you, Hulk."

Archer's eyes darkened at the name. He glared at Jack, then walked away, leaving Lily in the room with four men she'd never met before.

Silence followed Archer's departure until Daniel spoke up. "Sorry about that. Archer's nickname gets to him at times. Everyone's does. We shouldn't be dragging you into the middle of it."

Lily smiled at him. He was clearly the one who was in charge. He was tall, she noticed that when he walked in and almost hit his head. Granted, the ceilings were low in their 1970's building, but Daniel seemed twice her size. His long legs stretched out to the side, encased in dark jeans. His gray shirt brought out a silver tone in his dark eyes, eyes that took in everything around them. His skin was the same beautiful color as the walnut table they were sitting around.

Daniel rose from his seat and indicated Lily should sit.

"I'm fine. Thanks. I need to clean up the kitchen."

"We can help with that. You cooked, you shouldn't clean also."

"I don't mind."

"At least let me help then," he said, his deep voice soothing her and making her trust that he would help bring Jaymes back. "Tell me about Jaymes."

Lily smiled thinking about her best friend. "He's a great person. Always wants to help people. He volunteers at the community center teaching classes to the neighborhood. He's always so patient even though the people there always ask the same questions over and over again. He loves his job. He plays softball in a league over the summer, it just finished. He's just... you need to find him."

Lily teared up thinking about never seeing Jaymes again. She could convince herself before that he was just going to walk back in the door, but being confronted with a room full of muscle and government skills to find people, she was starting to doubt that she'd ever see her friend again.

Daniel patted her arm. "We're going to do everything we can."

Lily nodded and swiped the tears gathered on her lashes. She couldn't fall apart. She had a bunch of hungry men to feed. She couldn't help them find Jaymes, but she could make sure they were well fed.

"Thank you. I know Archer feels better with you guys here."

Jack snickered, but a slap echoed through the room before he yelled out. "What the hell was that for?"

Daniel turned around. "Knock it off. All of you. You're not children. Act like it."

"Yes sir," they all said in unison.

"You're good at that," Lily said.

Daniel winked at her, then asked, "Can we have permission to check out your place? Archer said it was broken into also. We'd like to get a look around there after we look around here. See if we can find anything."

Lily nodded and pointed to her purse hanging on the back of one of the chairs. Ryker, she thought, was sitting in the chair. He hadn't said anything so far.

"Dex, purse," Daniel barked.

Ryker got up and handed over the bag. Lily dug out her keys and gave them to Daniel. "The pink key. I'm in number nine, down one flight."

"Thanks. How are you?"

She shrugged. "Okay as I can be. My best friend is missing, my apartment was broken into and searched, and there are five men I've never met before trying to solve it all. It's a little surreal, to be honest."

Daniel smiled, white teeth offsetting his dark skin. He was definitely the leader, and it was easy for Lily to see why. He took charge without making a person feel like they were being controlled. She handed over her keys to him without a second thought. He was the kind of guy she would trust with her life. Between him and Archer, nothing would happen to her.

"We can be a bit overwhelming, but we mean well. Can you think of anyone that might have taken Jaymes? His truck is outside, right?"

Lily nodded. "Yeah, it is. But I don't know who would have taken him. He's not small so I doubt it was one person, but how did they take him without anyone noticing? And why aren't they asking for something?"

"Have you talked to his mom?"

Lily shook her head. "I didn't want to worry her."

Daniel nodded. "I understand. At this point, I think it's worthwhile to call her. She could know something we don't know. I'll ask Archer. Thanks, Lily. You've been a huge help. And sorry about the guys. They're all good men, just a little competitive, especially when it comes to women."

Lily smiled. "It's fine. I know neither of them mean anything by it."

Daniel snickered. "I'm not so sure about that. Archer doesn't get that worked up over a woman. Ever."

Daniel left her standing there, wondering why Archer cared who flirted with her.

"SHE'S PRETTY. Hell of a cook, too," Dunn said as he walked into the office.

Archer glared at him. "You gonna start with me, too?"

Dunn shook his head. "Nope. Just making conversation."

"Good. And keep your hands to your fucking self while you're at it."

Dunn huffed a laugh. "How long have you known her?"

"I got here yesterday."

Dunn's dark brows rose. "And that fast you're sniffing?"

"I'm not sniffing. She's best friends with my brother."

"Which she made perfectly clear means she's single. You're the one who argued that point."

Archer sighed. "Do you have anything for me besides shit, because I'm fresh out of caring right now. My brother's missing."

"Need you to call your mom."

"No," Archer said immediately. If he called his mom, he'd get a guilt trip about coming home. She didn't even know he was out yet, and he didn't want to tell her he was out and Jaymes was gone.

"She might have some information we need. Maybe someone called her."

Archer ran a hand down his face. Dunn was right, but he didn't like it. His relationship with his mother was tenuous at best. She never stood up for him with his father. She was meek and complacent and did anything he told her to do. Even after his father died, his mother never said a bad word about him, or challenged any of his decisions. Archer was perfectly happy to tell the asshole off, but his mother was always right there telling Archer to back off.

The last time Archer saw her was almost six years ago. He was on leave and decided to visit for a couple days. She spent the entire time treating him like a child who needed everything done for him instead of a man. He couldn't handle it and cut the trip short, lying that he got called back early and disappearing into a bottle and a woman.

Archer sucked in a breath and pressed the button to call his mom. He'd had the same phone number for as long as he'd had a cell phone, but she never bothered to enter names in her phone, so she answered with a confused, "Hello?"

"Hey, Ma."

"Hi, Jaymes. How are you, honey?"

"It's not Jaymes, Ma. It's Archer."

"Archer? Well, my goodness. How are you?"

"I'm good. I need to talk to you about Jaymes. Have you heard from him?"

She tsked, and he felt the guilt right through the phone. "We'll get to your brother. For now, tell me about you. When are you coming home? It's been too long since I've seen you."

"We can talk about that another time. I need to know about Jaymes."

"Archer Sinclair Ford. Your father did not raise you to speak to me that way."

"You're right. He didn't raise me at all. Focus. Jaymes. He's missing. Have you heard anything?"

The protest died on her lips with a gasp. "Jaymes is missing. What are you talking about? How do you know?"

"Have you heard from anyone?"

"No. Who would I have heard from? What happened?"

Archer pulled in a breath and tried to stay calm. His mother was as flighty as she was loyal to his father. She couldn't keep track of a thought if it killed her. "We're trying to figure out what happened. Have you heard anything? From Jaymes or someone asking about Jaymes over the last few days?"

"The only one who called me was his friend, Lily. Such a sweet girl. I think Jaymes has a thing for her. A crush. Do you kids still say that? She's a pretty girl, too. A little chubby, but she's pretty for a big girl."

"Lily's gorgeous, Ma. For any size. She's perfect how she is."

"I didn't know you knew her."

Archer sighed again. "I met her yesterday when I got here. I need to know—"

"Here? Are you in town?"

"Yes, Ma. Can we get back to Jaymes?"

"Why didn't you tell me you were coming to town? I would have fixed up your room for you. You don't need to stay in a hotel. I'll cook your favorite dinner. You can come over for dinner tonight."

"Ma!"

She gasped. "Archer. Don't yell at me. What's wrong with you?"

"Did anyone else ask you about Jaymes lately?"

"No. No one called. There was that nice man at church last weekend that asked about both of you, but that was a week ago."

"What man?" Archer demanded, his gut stirring.

"Oh, I don't know. He's new. Said his name was... oh, what was it? I can't remember. You should come to church today. He said he'd be back. I'll introduce you."

Archer traded a look with Dunn and closed his eyes. "Sure, Ma. I'd love to."

"Ooh, good. Now, mass starts at ten. Don't be late, Archer Sinclair Ford. You're not too old for a spanking."

"Okay, Ma." Archer took a deep breath and hung up, glaring at Dunn snickering.

"She's going to be interesting, isn't she?"

Archer rolled his shoulders and nodded. "My mother thinks my father hung the moon, and my brother hoisted him up on his shoulders. I'm just the speck on their shoes."

"She sounded pretty happy to hear from you. How long's it been since you've been home?"

"Almost six years."

Dunn whistled. "Damn. Even I'm not that bad. My mama'd kill me if I didn't visit at least every year."

"Is yours as crazy as mine?"

Dunn smiled and shook his head. "Nope. Mine's pretty great."

"Consider yourself lucky."

"I do. Now let's go to church."

Lily stood back while the guys changed into clothes they could wear to church. It shocked her when Jack stripped his shirt off in front of her and rummaged through his bag, but then the others followed suit and she nearly swallowed her tongue. Of course, none of them held a candle to Archer. His sculpted muscles had pink slashes across them, some artfully concealed by tattoos and others bright and angry. She couldn't take her eyes off him no matter how hard she tried. He was a work of art.

She was surprised he was going to church. Jaymes went once in a while, but he hated it. Their mom insisted on going every week and tried to talk Jaymes into it. He always said he had better things to do.

Liam set up his computer on the kitchen table and outfitted all of them with tiny microphones and cameras that stuck to their clothes and were invisible. They decided to leave Liam at the apartment with Lily to monitor what was going on and keep her safe. She started to protest that she didn't need a babysitter, but Archer shut her down with a look that said he wasn't going to argue the point.

When he was dressed, Archer nodded toward the bedroom. She glanced behind herself for whoever he was motioning to, but no one was there. He rose his eyebrows and smiled at her, and she followed him.

"Liam's a good guy," Archer said when they were in the relative private of Jaymes's bedroom. "You'll be safe with him."

"Isn't he a computer guy?"

Archer nodded. "He's also a trained SEAL with combat skills and sniper training. He's not someone I'd fuck with, but he is someone I'd trust. That's why I'm leaving him here with you."

Lily grinned. "Not Jack?"

Archer swore. "No. Not Jack. He's not allowed near you."

"You know you sound jealous, right?"

Archer speared her with a dark, possessive look. "Do I have a reason to be?"

Lily slowly shook her head.

"Good. Because it looked to me like you weren't staring at Jack out there."

"You took your shirt off because he did?"

Archer raised his eyebrows.

Lily laughed.

"You weren't laughing when you saw me."

Lily shook her head. "No. I wasn't."

"Let's go!" someone called from the other room.

"I gotta head out."

"Archer," Lily said as he walked away.

"Yeah?"

"Be careful."

He flashed her a grin and nodded. "Always."

8

———

ARCHER WAS PLAYING WITH FIRE. IT WASN'T A SMART decision, but he couldn't seem to stop himself from flirting with Lily.

He joined the rest of the team in their Sunday best, but he could feel the moment she walked into the room. His eyes went right to hers, drinking her in one more time before he left.

A knock on the door startled all of them. Daniel moved behind Archer and went to the door with him. They both pulled their Glocks from waistbands, ready to do damage if they needed to.

Archer peeked through the peephole and sighed. "It's Williams."

He opened the door as he tucked his gun away.

"I expected a better welcome than two of my own guys pulling guns on me," Williams said.

"Sorry, sir. We didn't know who was here. The door downstairs is supposed to be locked."

"I trained both of you to pick locks, so I'm not sure why

you're surprised I got past it. Would have gone through this one, too, but I thought I'd give you the courtesy of a knock."

"Thank you, sir. We didn't know you were coming."

"What's with the suits?"

"Ford talked to his mother. Said some guy asked about Jaymes and him last week at church. We're going to go check him out."

Williams nodded. "Good. No other leads?"

Archer shook his head. "No, sir."

"Who's here?"

"English is staying with Lily."

"Who's Lily?"

"Best friend of the target, sir," Dunn said. "Her place was searched also. Nothing there."

"You went back over it?"

Dunn nodded. "Yes, sir. You can check, too. I'd welcome the help."

Williams nodded sharply. "I'll do that while you're all gone. Got cameras?"

"English has us all hooked up. We're good to go, sir," Dunn said.

"Head out. Hopefully you find a path. We could use one. Sorry about your brother, Ford."

"Thank you, sir. And thank you for being here to help."

"No place I'd rather be."

Archer grinned at the familiar statement. It was one of the many things he admired about his CO. Nothing rattled him. He had an even head on him, even in the face of the worst disaster. His wife sent him a Dear John letter when they were knee deep in sand and bullets, and Williams still said there was no place he'd rather be. And they all knew it was the truth. Williams loved the SEALs. He'd given everything to the SEALs. And he did it happily.

Archer, Dunn, Jack, and Dex filed out the door. Archer caught Lily's eye and winked at her before he left.

Dunn led them to a black SUV parked on the other side of the small lot. It was closer to the other building, by design. If anyone was watching, it wouldn't be hard to find out who they were, but Dunn was trying.

Ryker Hamilton was Dex, short for Poindexter, to the rest of them. He enlisted in the Navy, but he would have been an officer if he'd chosen to go to college. He was one of the smartest people Archer had ever met. He could figure out just about anything, and his skills had gotten them out of more than a few jams along the way.

Jack had a way with people. If he wanted to, he could have you on your heels confessing all your sins, but Jack also had the ability to put people at ease. They wanted to be friends with Jack, which made him as deadly gathering info as he was with a long-range rifle in his hands.

Archer directed them to his childhood church, where his mom still faithfully attended mass. They parked in the back, out of sight but ready to go if they needed to get out in a hurry. Archer would have laughed at the way they all tucked guns in their holsters and covered them with jackets if it weren't for the fact that they were about to walk into his mom's church that way.

Dunn, Jack, and Dex followed Archer inside. He shook hands with the priest and found his mother in the same pew she'd always occupied halfway toward the front on the right.

"Hey, Ma," Archer said as he slid next to her. Cecelia Ford was a woman who took pride in her appearance. Archer had never seen her without makeup, even when he was a kid. Her dress was one Archer remembered, a fitted blue dress that fell past her knees. Her black heels were low and suitable for church. She was always careful to be appropriate. Drawing attention to yourself wasn't good. No one needed to know what went on inside a family except the family.

Hell, even the family didn't know what was going on sometimes. Archer had been left out too many times to count. His mother, father, and brother were peas in a pod. He was that little piece of spine that was on the outside, never a part of the crowd.

"Archer. It's good to see you. You're too skinny."

"Thanks, Ma. This is my XO, Daniel Dunn, and Ryker Hamilton and Jack Farrell, other Team members."

"Nice to meet you boys. Are you coming to dinner tonight?"

The guys tripped over each other to accept the invitation. Not that Archer blamed them. A peek inside the life of a teammate was something few SEALs were afforded. They came together as individuals and created a family on the front lines. Whatever family they had before barely existed to a SEAL.

"Thank you, Mrs. Ford. It's very kind of you," Dunn said. "Do you see the man who was asking about Jaymes?"

Archer shot him a glare, but Dunn ignored him. They were there for a reason. Archer knew it, but the last thing any of them needed was his mother going nuts in the middle of church.

Cecelia looked all around her and stopped when she was facing to the far right. "He's over there," she said in a normal voice. "Handsome man. Dark hair. Toward the back." Cecelia waved, and the man in question waved back with a smile.

"Need a closer look," a voice in Archer's ear told them.

"Later," Dunn replied. "The service is starting."

Archer and the others followed along with the rest of the

church. The movements were stiff and unfamiliar, but Archer participated as best he could.

When the music finally played and the priest made his retreat down the aisle, Archer searched out the man his mother waved to earlier. He was making his way through the crowd toward them.

"Incoming," he whispered before the man was there. He was of average height, a little pudgy around the middle. He looked like he was close to Cecelia's age, making Archer think it was as innocent as an old guy wanting to score.

"Hello again, Cecelia. How are you this week?" he asked.

"Good, good. How are you?"

"I'm doing well. I'm guessing this is Jaymes. He has your eyes."

Cecelia shook her head. "This is Archer. Jaymes is missing."

Archer stepped forward. "She means Jaymes couldn't make it today. Archer Ford."

"Nice to meet you, Archer. I'm Willie. Your mother talks about both you and your brother. I'm sorry I couldn't meet him as well. I figured you'd be the one who was harder to track down."

Archer nodded. "I am. Just home for a quick vacation. What do you do, Willie?"

He smiled and leaned back. "I just sold my hardware store. Retired now."

"Run financials," Dunn whispered to English listening in to their conversation.

"On it," English relayed.

"You know my mother's on a fixed income, right?"

Willie's smile faltered just enough for Archer to wonder if he was legit. "I'm not sure what that has to do with me.

Your mother's a beautiful woman. I'm just looking for a friend."

"That better be all you're looking for," Archer said, moving closer to him.

Cecelia slapped Archer's arm. "Get out of the way. You're not my husband. And I'm not getting another one," she said to Willie. "Friendship I can offer, but I'm faithful to my husband so if you have other ideas, I'm afraid you truly are barking up the wrong tree."

Willie smiled and tipped his hat, then turned and walked away.

"Well, I swear. Old men are even hornier than teenagers. I thought you and your brother were bad with all the sticky laundry I had to do. I'm not doing an old man's laundry."

Dunn, Jack, and Dex snickered, and Archer groaned. "Ma. Seriously?"

Cecelia shook her head. "Young men like them probably did the same thing. You all think we don't know, but we know what's going on. I'm just glad I never had to dig condoms out of the laundry. Although now that I think about it, I'm not sure that's a good thing either. You don't have kids running around, do you?"

"No, Ma. Jesus."

"Don't you take the Lord's name in vain."

"Sorry," Archer mumbled.

"Do you need anything else from me? I forgot to ask Willie why he wanted to know about you and Jaymes."

"It's okay. I think we got all we need."

"Sticky socks and all," English whispered in his ear.

Dunn, Jack, and Dex laughed again.

Assholes.

"Don't forget about dinner tonight, honey. I want more

of a chance to catch up with you, but we have bingo in twenty minutes, and I need to get over there," Cecelia said.

"Yeah, okay."

"See you tonight."

"Bye, Ma," Archer said, kissing her cheek.

She shuffled to her car. Archer watched until she got in and pulled out of the lot, then turned to the guys.

"Anything?"

"Guy's clean," English said. "Not even a damn parking ticket. I doubt he's the one we're looking for. Sounds like he was just trying to get in your Ma's pants."

"Fuck you, English."

The four of them laughed at Archer. Dunn and Dex walked off toward the SUV. Archer followed behind them and scanned the lot. Jack walked silently by his side, his gaze tracking the same spots Archer's were. There was something he was missing, but he couldn't figure out what it was. He had an odd feeling. Like there was an answer right in front of him, but it wasn't obvious.

Archer got in the SUV and sat silently while the others talked. The guy was coincidental, but that didn't mean there was more to it than him. There had to be something else that could lead them to Jaymes. Something he was missing.

He wasn't a good brother. He hadn't been his whole life, and it was going to cost Jaymes if Archer couldn't pull his head out of his ass and figure out what was going on.

When the guys got back to Jaymes's apartment, Lily breathed a little easier. No, Archer didn't bring Jaymes back with him, but he was back safe. She considered it a win.

Archer asked Williams if he found anything they missed

in Lily's apartment. She already knew the answer, but she didn't want to miss anything else. It was hard enough sitting in the room while the other guys communicated through their invisible earplugs. She wanted to know what was going on.

"A small bug. Base of a lamp in the living room. No way to tell how long it's been there, but it looked new."

"Any prints?"

Williams shook his head. "Nothing."

"Dammit."

Williams clapped Archer on the shoulder. "We'll figure this out. Tell me more about your brother. You never talked about him."

Guilt flashed across Archer's face before he could guard against it. The same expression was there whenever she said something about Jaymes that Archer didn't know. She wasn't trying to make things harder for him, but anyone who knew either of them knew they weren't close. It was worse than she thought if Archer's CO didn't even know Jaymes existed.

"Honestly, sir, I didn't know him well. There's four years, almost five, between us. We haven't been close since we were kids. I've barely spoken to him in years."

Williams pulled up a file on his phone. "Background check shows employment history and school. Four years Navy."

"What? No. My brother wasn't in the Navy."

Panic filled Lily's throat. Archer's eyes swung to hers. He saw the truth there, and she regretted not telling him earlier. He wouldn't understand that it was Jaymes's secret to share, not hers, and she didn't feel it was her place.

Now that choice was taken from both of them.

Williams' eyebrows tugged together as he frowned at the phone. "That's what it says here. Look."

Archer took the phone and scrolled through the data about his brother. He shook his head slightly. "Will you send that to me?"

Williams nodded and took his phone back. He keyed the email in and a ding echoed in Archer's pocket. "I take it there's a lot you didn't know about your brother," Williams said sympathetically.

Archer nodded. "You could say that. Excuse me, sir." Archer crooked a finger at Lily to follow him to the back of the apartment.

"I'm sorry I didn't tell you. He didn't want you to know," Lily said as soon as the door shut behind them.

"Why not?"

"You're his big brother. You're his hero. He'd never admit it, but he worshipped you. Still does, I think. He wanted to be like you, but he knew he needed a degree. He went to OCS and wanted to be a SEAL. He quit after only a couple weeks. He never wanted you to know he failed."

"Becoming a SEAL is one of the hardest things anyone can do. I'm kind of impressed he even tried, but if he only went to be like me, I'm not surprised he rang out."

Lily didn't like Archer implying that Jaymes wasn't good enough. He was strong and kind and amazing. He could be anything he wanted to be, and damn Archer for saying he couldn't.

"You don't know anything about him. He could have done it. He's just as tough as you are. Don't you dare say he's not good enough."

Archer grinned at Lily's outburst, which only served to piss her off even more.

"And don't laugh at me. Why do you think so little of him? No wonder you two never talk. I wouldn't want to talk to you if you treated me like a worthless piece of shit either."

Lily moved to shove past Archer, but he blocked her way. All evidence of his humor was gone. His eyes blazed when she looked up at them. She saw the SEAL, not the man, and backed away.

"First of all, I'm not laughing at you. You're protective of him. I might be a little jealous of that, but I was laughing because you misunderstood me. Which brings me to my second point. If Jaymes wanted to be a SEAL and was willing to sacrifice everything to get there, he could have done it. I've never known my brother to fail when he really wanted to succeed. If he was doing it as some misguided attempt to impress me, that's why he failed. He didn't want it bad enough. And trust me when I tell you you have to want it. You don't become a SEAL because you wake up one day and decide to be. It's months of training in the worst conditions you can possibly imagine. I thought I was going to die, and prayed for death, more times in the six months I spent in Coronado than any other time in my life. You can't half-ass that job. So it sucks that he didn't make it, but all I was saying was he failed before he ever started if he was only doing it because of me."

He took a step closer to her. Lily backed up again, her ass hitting the edge of Jaymes's desk.

She lifted her eyes to his. Anger blended with desire and something else, something that told her what she was thinking was a really bad idea.

But in that moment, she didn't care. She just had to feel his lips against hers. Nothing else mattered.

9

———

Lily's expression melted from one of anger to one of heat in less than a breath. Archer's brain registered what was going on seconds before she leapt at him.

He caught her easily and was going to set her away, but then she wrapped her legs around his hips. His hands automatically went to her thighs to hold her steady, and he was lost.

They stared at each other for a long moment. The room heated up around them. Her fingers teased the short hairs on the back of his neck. His cock rose to a painful height. He couldn't deny he wanted her for another second.

He leaned down the same time she lifted up, and their lips collided. He froze for a second, panic settling into him. Did he read her wrong somehow? She seemed like she wanted to kiss him, but the second their lips touched, she stopped.

He eased back, staring at her closed eyes and pinched lips. "Lily?"

"Why'd you stop?"

"I thought—"

"Stop thinking and kiss me."

"Yes, ma'am," he said, diving in again.

She responded to him eagerly, darting her tongue out to taste his lips before sucking his bottom lip between her teeth for a nibble.

Archer growled and spun them. He backed her up until her back hit the door, then made good use of his hands as he pried her lips apart with his tongue.

He cupped her curvy ass with one hand, testing the feel of her soft flesh in his palm. She liked that if the whimpering was any indication. His other hand reached for her hair. He'd been dying to know if it was as soft as it looked.

Her tongue slid along his, and she held on to his shoulders. She tasted like her cupcakes, chocolate with a burst of sweetness. Archer growled and flexed his hips to stroke her sex. She whimpered, that same sexy sound she made when she got herself off the night before, and he did it again.

He tugged her hair until her head fell back against the door, then trailed his tongue down her neck. She wriggled against him when he nipped her collarbone.

"Oh, God," she whispered. Her hips moved against him, sliding her jeans covered center over his cock.

He was gone. The months away from civilization combined with the grief of losing his best friend amplified every sensation. He hadn't held a woman in far too long, but this one... She was different. She was one who would make his life messy. She wasn't a faceless woman from a bar. She wasn't a woman he would walk away from after he pulled his pants back up and never see again. She was best friends with his brother. It didn't matter that he hadn't seen his brother in years, Lily would always be there.

The only thing he hated about that was the knowledge that she'd be in his brother's life, and not his.

Suddenly, the thought of not having her was harder to swallow than the thought of having her and walking away.

He let her drag his mouth back to hers and devour him. She kissed with her whole body, from her hands that held his head in place to her lips and tongue that drove him mad to her legs that tightened around him every time he did something she liked. He loved a woman who made kissing about more than just their lips.

A knock had them jumping back. The sound echoed through the hollow door, but Archer knew whoever was on the other side was also knocking to piss him off. They knew exactly what was going on inside that room.

"What?" Archer demanded.

"Wanted an update. Need to talk through all this from the beginning," Dunn's voice came through.

"Give us a minute."

"Sure thing," Dunn said, half-laughing.

Archer waited until he was sure no one was outside the door, then pressed Lily against it again. "We're not done here."

"I hope not. I still have clothes on."

"I'm no good for you, Lily."

She rolled her eyes. "This is the part where you think I'm trying to get involved. You're hot, and I haven't had sex in far too long. That's all this is. Two adults with chemistry. When you find Jaymes, you're going to leave. I know that. I'm not walking into this picturing white picket fences and two-point-five kids. I'm happy with my life, and I'm not looking to change it right now. Except for the part where I get a few orgasms out of the deal, we'll be strangers again in a few days."

Archer didn't like the way she dismissed him so easily, but it eased his anxiety over breaking her heart. She was the only woman he'd known who Archer knew would weather a broken heart the same way as a soldier.

She'd pick herself up and move the fuck on.

The thought didn't sit well with him, but it was the only option.

LILY WALKED out of the room on shaky legs. Being so close to Archer was a potent combination of desire and desperation, with a little bit of what-the-fuck-am-I-thinking thrown in.

She meant what she said about Archer leaving and not being interested in more than a few days of sex, or whatever he was interested in. She didn't really care as long as her overall orgasm counter added a few ticks to it.

Even better if they were supplied by someone other than her.

The guys all looked up when Lily walked in but quickly busied themselves with computers and conversations and anything that didn't require looking at her. She felt Archer behind her before he slid a huge, warm hand down her spine and gave her hip a squeeze.

If anyone understood how hard everything that was happening was, it was definitely him. He loved Jaymes and was just as scared as she was, and just as thrown by the insane chemistry between them if she had to guess. Jaymes knew Archer as well as Archer knew Jaymes, which meant Lily really didn't know much about the guy she had her legs wrapped around just a few seconds ago.

"What's up?" Archer asked, moving beyond her to the mass of muscle that claimed Jaymes's living room.

"We need to start over. We're not finding anything that gives us a direction. We need some clues, and you two are the only ones who can give them to us." Daniel was definitely the leader of the group. He took charge and built a plan. Lily was happy he was there to find her friend.

Six pairs of eyes swung to Lily. She usually hid from male attention, knowing they preferred someone with less fluff in their cupcakes, but this was for Jaymes. None of those guys were looking at her like she was anything other than a source of information.

"Lily, will you tell us everything you know?" Archer asked, motioning for her to come closer.

Lily nodded and moved toward him. Instead of using him for support, she sat on the couch near Daniel. He scooted over to give her space, with a discrete nod at Archer, and started asking questions.

"Where does Jaymes work?"

"Morrison Chemical Corporation."

"What does he do there?"

"He's the IT manager. He handles everything with all the networks they run."

"What exactly does that mean?"

"He's responsible for the network inside and outside the plant. He makes sure everything stays running. They have servers that store all their data but also that keep the plant running. He has to maintain all of it."

"What does the company do?"

"They make nitroglycerin."

The six men in the room exchanged glances.

"For what purpose?" Daniel asked.

"Isn't it used for heart patients?"

Daniel nodded. "It is. But it can be used in explosives, too. It was originally used in dynamite. They discovered its use to help heart disease almost thirty years after it was first used as an explosive."

"Wait, something that helps people with bad hearts is used in dynamite?"

Everyone nodded. "Exactly. It's diluted, of course, but it's the same thing. They could be after his access."

Lily sat there as the room went nuts trying to dig up information about Morrison and everyone who worked there. They asked her for names of other people he worked with and wanted more information about the company. It all happened so fast her head spun.

When they all dove into the phone and computers and conversations on their own, Lily leaned back against the couch and thought about what just happened. Was it possible someone wanted something from Morrison? Were they really after Jaymes because he could get them an explosive?

The thought of something like that happening made Lily sick. She didn't want to imagine Jaymes being forced to do something like that. Or anyone else.

Archer lowered himself to the couch next to her and rested a hand on her thigh.

"Is that what's really happening? Someone is trying to blow something up?"

Archer took a deep breath. "It sounds reasonable. I'm not sure why they need a computer guy for it, though. That's the part that doesn't make much sense to me. One of the lower-level employees would be easier to bribe. Especially one with a family. Wave some money under his nose and threaten his family, and these people could have gotten anything they wanted. Why Jaymes?"

The back of Lily's throat tingled. A wave of nausea rose from her stomach and filled her mouth with saliva. She tried to swallow it down, to push away the thoughts, but it was coming up whether she wanted it to or not.

Lily shoved off the couch and bolted for the bathroom with a hand clamped over her lips. She tasted the putrid substance, trying to choke it down and needing to get it out at the same moment. She slammed the bathroom door shut and spun, barely making it to the toilet before she emptied her stomach.

The heaving burned her throat, bile clinging to every surface inside her. Her nose filled with the scent. Tears streamed down her cheeks, and she just wanted to sit down and cry.

When her body was finally empty, she slumped to the floor. She reached to flush the toilet and clear the room of the evidence of her weakness, then forced herself to stand and clean up. She swished some overly minty mouthwash and dabbed her cheeks with a wet tissue. She wasn't perfect, but she was better. She just had to stop thinking about threats and dynamite and her missing friend.

Archer was on the other side of the door when Lily opened it. "Are you okay?"

She forced a smile and nodded. "I'm good. Sorry about that."

Lily walked past him and straight into the kitchen. She could use some fresh air, but in lieu of that, she'd cook.

Groceries were already getting low, but she had enough to make sausage and spinach stuffed shells for everyone. The guys talked and moved in the other room, but left her alone to cook. When she had lunch in the oven, she started on a fresh batch of muffins. Brownies, too. If the way they destroyed the cupcakes she made the day before were any indication, she'd need both muffins and brownies to get through the night with these guys.

An hour later, Lily pulled the stuffed shells out of the oven and put the muffins and brownies in. The rich smells made her stomach growl as though she hadn't eaten in far longer than the couple hours it had been since breakfast.

"Lunch is ready if you guys are hungry," she told the group.

"What'd you make me?" Jack asked, the first one in the room. "If it's half as good as those cupcakes, I'm not sharing."

Lily laughed, finally feeling more like herself. Cooking and laughter did that for her. She knew who she was if she could be in the kitchen and having fun with friends. Jack would disappear as quickly as Archer, but for the moment, she considered him a friend.

"Sorry, brownies and muffins are still in the oven. I made sausage and spinach stuffed shells. There's cheese in them, but I like to add a little extra something. Hopefully you like it. I need to do some shopping so if you have any requests, let me know."

Jack took the plate Lily offered him and grinned at her. "I have lots of requests, but I'll eat just about anything."

"That's true," Archer said, joining them. "He's like a human garbage can."

Jack smiled. "Food is food. When you're hungry enough, you don't care what you eat. Just that you get to."

Lily wondered at the meaning behind Jack's words, but he moved away, settling on the couch to eat while the others filed through the kitchen.

Lily stood in the kitchen eating her lunch. The couch was full, as was the dining room table with all Liam's computers and other equipment. Lily had no idea where everyone was going to sleep. She'd offered up her apartment, but that wouldn't take care of all of them. Plus the two more that were supposedly on their way.

The guys chatted as they ate, acting like nothing unusual

was going on. It struck Lily that for them, it wasn't unusual. They were used to this. They'd been in the same situation more times than she'd ever imagine.

She just hoped they had a good track record.

"You okay?" Archer asked, leaning against the counter next to her after he rinsed his plate and set it in the dishwasher.

Lily nodded. "I guess. I feel so useless right now. You guys are all doing your SEAL thing, and I'm just cooking."

Archer grinned. "Every person who's ever been in the military, any branch, any time, will all tell you the same thing."

"What's that?"

"That the person who provides the food is one of the most important people."

Lily grinned, feeling marginally better. Everyone had to eat, and if she could provide that for them, it was more time they could all spend searching and strategizing.

"Ford," Brady said.

Lily smiled at the man the others followed without question. He took her keys when Archer was at church and searched her apartment again. She was hopeful he'd find something, but when all he came back with was a tiny bug, she was both disappointed and disturbed. He was equally upset on her behalf.

"Yes, sir," Archer said, turning from her.

"I'm going to check into a hotel. If anyone wants somewhere else to stay, it's on me. Lily was generous enough to offer her place as well, but I wanted to make sure you knew I was willing to provide housing if need be also."

"Thank you, sir."

"If Lily will get me a list, I'll do a grocery run before I come back."

"Thank you, Brady," Lily said. "You don't have to do that."

He nodded, his military stiff composure slipping for just a second. Vulnerability and compassion sneaked in. "It's the least I can do. You've been feeding us all day, and I have no doubt you will continue to do so. It's the least I can do."

"You're here and helping. That's enough, sir," Archer insisted.

Brady shook his head. "Let me help. I'm sorry this is happening to you. You don't need one more thing to worry about. And I don't think it's safe for Lily to be out on her own, so it only makes sense."

"Are you sure you should be alone?"

Brady shook his head. "No one knows who I am. They obviously know you, but I'm just an old man, invisible to the world. No one will bother me."

"He has a point, Lil," Archer said.

Lily nodded. "Thank you, Brady. I'll get a list to you shortly. When are you leaving?"

Brady shrugged. "Most hotels don't allow check-in until three, so any time after that."

"Are you coming to dinner at my mom's?" Archer asked.

Brady nodded. "Wouldn't miss it."

10

———

"How are things going?" he asked the first guy, the taller one. He looked like he could be Hispanic, or maybe Italian. He didn't know his name. He didn't really care. These guys were a means to an end. They weren't important, and never would be.

"Guy's a pain in the ass. Keeps asking for things he says he needs."

"Like what?"

"He said he needs to get online. Research or some such shit."

"I told you no internet," he said harshly. If everything fell apart because these stupid fucks didn't know how to follow orders, he'd kill them with his bare hands instead of the bullets he had for them.

He hadn't come this far to fail in the last step of the whole plan. Two years of hard work. No. Fuck no.

"We told him that. He said he had to check something."

"Did you let him?"

The guy shook his head, dark, greasy hair flopping over his shoulder. He was little better than scum, but that was what money could buy you. Jaymes Ford hadn't been easy to come by, but he wasn't the kind of guy who took to trades.

Not that they hadn't tried. He was asked to look the other way, and refused. So they had no choice, really. He knew too much, and they couldn't risk him alerting anyone.

"Hey, Oscar, this guy said—" The other flunky entered the room, his laughter dying on his lips as he realized they weren't alone.

"Don't stop there. I'm dying to know what he said."

This one was smaller, stocky. The kind of guy who'd be good in a fight because of his compact form. He swallowed and traded a look with Oscar. Oscar shook his head just enough to be suspicious.

"What did he say?"

"He said he has a cute girlfriend."

He shook his head. "I don't think that's what he really said. Why don't you try again?"

The guy swallowed. "He said he could get us everything we needed if we let him go."

"And what did you tell him?"

"What you said, boss. That all we need from him is the code. The one we told him to change."

"And did he give it to you yet?"

The guy shook his head. "No. It's not done yet."

"When will it be done?"

The guy shrugged. "He doesn't know."

"Then maybe he needs a little motivation to finish up."

He grabbed a mask from the shelf and slid it over his face. He couldn't risk being identified by him after all this was over. Not that he planned to let the guy go, but shit happened. He knew enough to know he couldn't plan for everything.

He walked into the room and closed the door behind

him. The metal squeaked and screamed at the pressure of being closed.

Jaymes turned around, startled by the sound, then jumped when he saw him there. "Who are you?"

"I'm the guy who planted a bug in your girlfriend's apartment. She's pretty. I can see why you like her."

"You stay away from her," Jaymes threatened low and deadly like he'd actually do something about it.

Funny, since he was chained to the metal chair he sat in. The only time he got out of that chair was to take a piss, during which time he was chained to one of the idiots put in charge of guarding him, or sleeping, when he was chained to the bed.

It was really rather nice of them to give him a bed.

"I don't know if I can stay away from her. A pretty girl like her. Maybe if you can't finish the job, she will. The boys would love to have her down here. Brighten up the place, I'm sure."

"What do you want?"

"I want the fucking program! I want you to finish what you started. And I want to see everything destroyed."

Jaymes glared at him, his eyes narrowing. He was a fighter, that much was obvious. But he knew he was defeated. He had no choice. Not if he wanted to protect his girlfriend.

"I'll do it," Jaymes finally said. "Just stay away from her."

He laughed. "I'll do whatever I want. Especially if you don't do as I say. You have twenty-four hours."

He turned and walked away, ignoring Jaymes Ford's protests that it wasn't enough time. He didn't fucking care. It had to be enough time. If not, Lily Scott would run out of time.

ARCHER LEANED back in his chair and smiled. He wasn't expecting to enjoy the dinner at his mom's house, but his buddies made it bearable. Them and Lily. She charmed everyone with her smile and her quick wit, and she dragged his mother into every conversation.

Archer knew his mom appreciated that. They were obviously close, which left him feeling a little guilty, but he could always change that. He was in DC, but there wasn't anything keeping him there. He hated growing up in Niagara Falls, but without his father around, life was different.

He didn't want to think about the fact that his father wasn't the only family member missing.

How would Jaymes take it when he came back and found Archer in his world. Lily made it sound like Jaymes worshipped him, but hero worship only went so far. Usually when a person met their heroes, it was a disaster. Heroes never lived up to the expectations of the people who wanted to know them. Jaymes would come back and find Archer in his mind was a hell of a lot better than Archer in reality.

As long as he found Jaymes and brought him back.

"Thank you for dinner, Mrs. Ford," Dex said. "We appreciate you inviting us all over tonight."

Dex had a way with the ladies. Always had. He could sweet talk his way out of anything, and he frequently did. Archer found it humorous that he was using his charms on his mother, but whatever. After the display at church that morning, he knew for sure his mother wasn't going to take anyone home.

Archer didn't understand her loyalty to his father. He'd never done anything to deserve it. He wasn't a horrible father to Jaymes, but he certainly wasn't a great one with Archer.

Life could have been worse between the walls of his childhood home. He was never abused, but he was definitely treated as the child who was less. Less intelligent, less important, less everything. All the times growing up that Archer wished he could be somewhere else, he never imagined where his freedom would take him.

The second he was old enough, he joined the Navy and became a SEAL. He was just starting to find himself there, and feel like he deserved to belong, and he was given his freedom again.

"You'll all have to come over again sometime," Cecelia said. "I only wish all of you had made it other times. The only person Archer ever brought home was that boy, Rodney. Why isn't he here?"

The room fell silent.

A vision of Rodney filled Archer's head. Blond hair matted on one side with blood. Vacant eyes staring up at the sky. Legs turned at a funny angle. The smell of gunpowder and stale air, mixed with the unmistakable scent of death and the metal tinge of blood.

Archer's throat dried up. He struggled to get air in his lungs. Panic slid up his spine and choked him.

He fucking hated panic attacks. He didn't have many, but when he was blindsided with the reminder of Rodney, he felt like his feet were kicked out from under him.

"We lost Rodney, ma'am," Williams said calmly.

Archer could feel them all watching him, waiting to see what he would do. Guilt weighed heavily on him. Rodney didn't have much family. His parents died years ago, shortly after Rodney and Archer joined the Teams. When they had breaks, Rodney and Archer were a pair. They hit up the bars together, picked up women together, took vacations together.

One of the few times Archer went home, Rodney asked to tag along. He'd never seen Niagara Falls and said a giant fucking waterfall sounded like heaven compared to the endless dessert they spent most of their time in. They stayed with his mother and Rodney loved her. She treated him like she did Jaymes and doted on him. Archer was surly and jealous, but he took it.

Rodney never went home with him after that. They got into a fight about it. Archer regretted being an ass, but he couldn't get over the fact that he was never the best. No matter what he did, he was always second place.

The next time Archer went home, Rodney took a trip to the Grand Canyon to see another one of the wonders of the world. He met Monica there, and came back to the Teams half in love.

They had their rough times, but Rodney worshipped her. She was everything he ever wanted in a woman, and he couldn't wait to marry her.

Until Archer shot him in the back of the head and stole that chance from them.

"I'm so sorry," Cecelia said. "He was such a sweet man. What happened to him?"

"I'm sorry, but that's classified," Williams said.

The subject changed, and Archer was finally able to breathe again. He excused himself a minute later, needing some fresh air to fix his head.

The backyard wasn't the place he wanted to be, but he wasn't stupid enough to go out front. The back was fenced in and no one would get back there without him knowing it.

Archer moved to the edge of the yard where the old soccer goal still sat. Grass was slightly longer around the rusted metal frame. A deflated ball rested at the back of the net. Archer wanted to break the thing with his bare hands, just tear it apart, but it wouldn't do any good. Letting his anger get the better of him was what got him into the biggest messes of his life, not out of them.

Footsteps swished through the grass and prompted Archer to turn.

"Sorry about that, Ford."

"Thank you, sir."

Williams was silent for a few minutes. "Are you doing okay with all that?"

Archer nodded. "Shrinks cleared me."

Williams was silent for a minute. "That's not what I meant. It's not easy losing a brother."

Archer snorted. "Or two."

Williams nodded. "I didn't even know you had a brother."

Archer shrugged. "I wasn't close to him growing up."

Williams nodded again.

Archer let the silence fill the space between them. He appreciated that Williams would let him stay silent and think, and not judge him for it. He needed that.

"Your mom was getting dessert out. She said apple pie is your favorite."

Archer huffed a laugh. "It's Jaymes's favorite."

Williams laughed. "Well, she was one for two."

"Yeah. Par for the course."

Williams clapped him on the back and walked inside. Archer followed a few seconds later so he could choke down some apple pie and pretend he loved it.

He'd just grab an extra of Lily's brownies when they got home.

Not home. Back to Jaymes's place.

"How long are you in town?" Cecelia asked Archer when they made their way to the door.

Lily didn't want to think about the answer to that question. Everything depended on how long it would take to find Jaymes. If they could find Jaymes.

Williams and Ryker searched Mrs. Ford's house during dinner. They didn't tell her what they were doing, so Lily was on lookout for her. She kept her talking while the guys searched the place. She was more than a little disappointed that they didn't find anything. It would have been more of a shock if they had, but still, she hoped.

"Hopefully not more than a few days. I should be gone by the end of the week," Archer said.

"Well, you should all come back. I have bible study on Tuesday and my support group on Wednesday. How about Thursday?"

Archer wanted to say no. Lily could see it in his eyes. The resignation. The determination. He wasn't in Mrs. Ford or Jaymes's lives because he had no interest in being in them.

Lily felt bad for him. She wasn't crazy about her crazy mother and her endless parade of husbands, but she loved her mother. She was a part of her life, from a few hundred miles away. She couldn't imagine being so separated from her mom that she didn't want to see her when she was in town.

Of course, Lily also didn't visit unless she was going to see her mother, but that was beside the point.

"We'd love to," Lily answered for Archer.

"We will?"

Lily nodded. "Absolutely. It'll be great. Let me know what I can bring this time."

Mrs. Ford grinned. "You know you don't have to bring anything."

Lily shook her head. "That's besides the point. You know I love to cook. I want to contribute."

"Well, thank you, Lily. I'll let you know when I decide on a menu for the night."

"Thanks. We'll see you then, Mrs. Ford."

The rest of the guys thanked her for the meal and filed out of the small house. They piled into dark SUVs and headed back to their homes for the night. It was all so covert and odd to Lily. Driving around in rented SUVs with a bunch of men who could take down any threat.

The two guys who showed up that afternoon decided to take Brady up on the offer to get a hotel room when they saw how crowded Jaymes's apartment was. Archer introduced them as Rocky and Slade, but Lily was pretty sure those weren't their real names.

The other six of them went to the apartment. They all trudged up the steps to Jaymes's apartment, the day catching up to everyone. Lily wanted nothing more than a bed to collapse into, but she had no idea if she'd get one.

"Hey Lily," Jack said as soon as they walked in. "Do you have a couch I can crash on? This one smells like Dex's farts."

Dex gave him a one-finger salute but didn't argue.

Lily laughed. "I do. If you think it's safe to be there."

The guys traded looks and nodded as though they were sharing a brain and made a decision at the same time.

"It'll be fine. Williams got the bug. I'm just not sure I like the idea of Jack down there with us," Archer whispered in her ear.

"Us?" Lily squeaked.

Archer slid an arm around her waist and pulled her close to him. "I said we weren't done, Lily. I planned to make good on that tonight."

Heat and desire raced down Lily's spine and settled between her thighs. She nodded and licked her lips.

"Grab your shit. It's time for bed."

"It's only— Oh. Okay."

Lily left to collect her bags, shoving everything she could find quickly into them. She was back in the living room and ready to go within seconds.

Archer and Jack had their bags at the door. The three of them walked down the flight of stairs and into Lily's apartment. It was still a mess. The thought of someone being in there gave her the creeps, but what bothered her even more was the sheet of paper taped to her fridge.

STOP LOOKING OR WE'LL BRING YOU TO HIM.

11

———————

ARCHER AND JACK DREW THEIR GUNS AND MOVED THROUGH
the entire apartment, checking everything. When he got
back to the kitchen, Lily hadn't moved. She was trembling.

"Does this mean what I think it means?" she asked, fear
and anger a strange combination in her voice.

Archer nodded. "It means they're going to take you if we
don't stop looking for him."

She stuck her chin out and glared up at him. "Fuck
them. I'm not scared."

Archer tugged her against him and breathed her in. She
was tough. Tougher than anyone he knew. Hell, there were
SEALs that weren't that strong without repeated exercises to
teach them how to be.

But this woman, this feisty brunette, she was ready to
take on whoever she had to for her best friend.

"Hopefully it won't come to that," Archer said.

Jack called Dunn and Williams to update them on the
note left on Lily's fridge while Archer got Lily a glass of
water and led her to the couch.

"This isn't strong enough," she declared. "I have vodka in the freezer."

"Drink it anyway. I'll get your vodka next."

Lily sipped the water dutifully. She stared off at a spot on the far wall, not moving.

Archer understood how she felt. Violated. Terrified. Pissed off. He was all the same things. And his protective instincts were clouding everything else. He wasn't going to let anyone touch her. If that meant keeping a hand on her until the threat was neutralized, he was the man for the fucking job.

He poured her a double vodka and traded her for the water. He sipped the water while she downed the vodka. She hissed at the burn and shook her head, then handed him back the glass.

"Better?"

Lily glared up at him. "No. Someone was in my home. More than once. They're threatening me. How am I supposed to be okay?"

Archer sat next to her and pulled her against his side. "This shouldn't be happening to you."

Lily shook her head against his shoulder. "It shouldn't be happening at all. Why is it? What is this all about?"

Archer sucked in a breath. "I wish I knew. It doesn't make sense that they would grab him of all the people at his company. They had to need something else from him. There has to be something else he's involved in or knows about that makes him the best candidate."

"Wait," Lily said, sitting up. "What do you mean?"

Every square inch of Archer went on alert. She figured something out. Something that was going to help. "I mean, if all they want is access to the plant, they don't need him. They're not going to target a manager of a department when they know he's going to be easier to notice is missing. They're going to go after someone with a poor attendance record, someone no one will think twice about not showing up one day. That's not Jaymes."

Lily shook her head slowly and stared off into the distance. Archer waited for her to say something, to share her revelation with him.

"A few months ago, Jaymes worked on a different project. I didn't think about it because it's been a little while, but it was all pretty secret. He didn't tell me much, but I helped him with some of the coding."

"What was the project?"

"It was something for the power plant."

"Oh, shit."

Lily swallowed. "That's what I was afraid you'd say."

"Tell me everything, Lily."

LILY DIDN'T KNOW MUCH about the project, but she shared every tidbit she could remember. Jaymes was redesigning the program that controlled how much water the power plant brought in from the Niagara River. Water came in from the river and was stored in a massive man-made lake downstream where it was released as needed to generate power for the area.

The power plant was massive, one of the biggest in the entire state. Shutting it down could be catastrophic for the area, even deadly if explosives were involved. The area surrounding the plant was residential and commercial, and densely populated.

"Who hired him to write the new program?"

"The power plant. Their program got corrupted

somehow and their IT manager was out on maternity leave. The other people in the department couldn't code an entire program quickly enough, so they reached out. Someone there knew one of Jaymes's bosses and they agreed to let him work there for a few weeks."

"If this has anything to do with the power plant, they could be looking to do anything from take out the plant to blow up the city."

"I know," Lily said softly.

Archer and Jack traded a look and called up to the others in Jaymes's apartment. They relayed everything Lily told them over the speakerphone and everyone jumped into action.

Lily watched as Jack checked and re-checked the arsenal of guns he had in his bag next to her couch. Archer and Liam talked so fast they weren't even speaking English anymore. It was some sort of shorthand that had her head spinning. Daniel and Ryker carried on a conversation in the background, the timbre of their voices barely audible over the clack of Liam's keyboard and Archer's voice.

When they hung up, Jack took the paper from the fridge upstairs to see if they could figure out anything about who left it. Archer guided Lily to her feet and into her bedroom.

He closed the door behind them and pulled her into his arms. She held on to him, letting him support her. She didn't like relying on other people, but she was terrified. She tried to be strong for Jaymes, but she couldn't do it anymore. Having someone to lean on sounded damn good.

Even better would be someone to lose herself in.

She tilted her head back and lifted onto her toes to kiss Archer. Surprise widened his eyes before their lips met, but he immediately pulled back.

Disappointment and embarrassment flooded Lily. She

stepped away and turned to busy herself with something, anything so she didn't have to look at Archer. After the blows she'd felt all day, rejection was the last straw. She could not let him see her cry.

"Lily."

She shook her head. "It's fine. I misunderstood what was going on here."

"Look at me."

She shook her head again. "You can go upstairs and help the rest of the guys. I'm just going to get some sleep."

"Dammit, Lily. Look at me."

She huffed and spun, not bothering to wipe her eyes. He wanted to see her, he could see all of her. Fuck him for making her feel like she wasn't good enough when he spent all day saying he wanted her.

"Shit. I didn't mean to make you cry."

She laughed mirthlessly. "You didn't. This whole day did. I'm worn out and stressed out and scared out of my mind. I was thinking some good sex would help, but you're not interested anymore so don't worry about it."

"Jesus. That's not why I stopped you."

She snorted and moved around her bed to her dresser. She grabbed some pajamas, a pair of flannel pants and a tank top that wouldn't tangle in her sheets and choke her when she tossed and turned. There was no doubt that was all she'd do all night.

"Lily, I want you. I just don't want you to regret this. Emotions are high right now. You're scared and worried about Jaymes. I don't want to add something else for you to think about."

She rolled her eyes. Men always thought they were the center of the universe. That women couldn't function without a man around to tell them how to operate. He was an idiot if he thought she was getting attached just because she was emotional.

"It's fine. You're probably right. I'm a woman, so of course I'm incapable of having sex just to have sex. It has to be the start of something."

"Fuck, Lily. I didn't say that."

"You may as well have. That's the second time today you accused me of being unable to sleep with you and let you walk away. I'm sorry, but you're the only one who seems to be having trouble with that idea. So maybe we shouldn't sleep together, because I don't need some sexy badass alpha SEAL chasing off all the men I do want to have sex with one day."

Fury flared in his eyes, and a responding heat bloomed in her gut. Archer was hot when he was jealous. It wasn't Lily's intention, but she'd be lying if she said she didn't appreciate the hell out of the reaction.

"I really don't like you talking about sex with other men when you and I are standing next to a bed."

Lily rolled her eyes. "Nothing is going to happen with us, in that bed or any other bed. You're not interested. And I'm not a glutton for punishment. You don't want me, that's fine. You can stay here and protect me. I've got a sleeping bag somewhere in the closet. You can camp out in the living room with Jack."

Archer moved around the bed, getting closer to her with each step. Lily fought the urge to climb over the bed and escape, but it was her room, dammit. If anyone was going to leave, it was going to be him.

When he was close enough to reach her, he stopped. "I don't know what made you think I don't want you, but you're wrong. I don't want your fear to be the only reason you fuck me tonight. Because I can promise you that the only reason I plan to get in that bed and make you come so many times you can't breathe is because you drove me crazy from the second I first saw you in those tiny little pajamas. I wanted to strip you right there and trace your nipples with my tongue. I wanted to feel how wet you were when you threatened to slide under the table and suck my dick. I wanted to make you come when you climbed me in my brother's office. Never in every moment we've been together today or yesterday have I not wanted you."

"Then why did you push me away?" Lily asked. She had to know the answer, even if his words had her so close to an orgasm all he'd have to do was tell her to come and she probably would.

"I need to know you want to be with me, and not just anyone."

"Seriously? I thought that was a girl's line."

Archer shook his head slowly. "You're not that kind of girl. That's what turns me on about you. One of the many, many things."

Lily's eyes dropped to his pants where he stroked himself through his jeans. Her breath froze in her throat. He stroked himself again. She licked her lips, and he groaned.

"Lily."

"Huh?"

"Tell me you want me."

She nodded.

"Say the words, Lily."

"I want you, Archer. You're the only one I want right now."

"Thank fuck for that."

She was in his arms, her lips crushed against his, before she could take her next breath. Her hands were pinned between them, trapped against his chest and hers. One of his arms was clamped tightly around her back, but his other hand kneaded her ass, teasing her with how close he was to where she throbbed for him.

Lily finally worked her arms free. She reached into his jeans and wrapped her fingers around his cock. Long, hard, and magnificent. She couldn't wait to get her lips on it.

Archer jerked in her hand, pulling away from her. She was stuck there, so he couldn't go far. He pulled away from their kiss and swore.

"This should be slow, but you've got me so fucking horny I can barely breathe. You need to stop touching me."

"You feel so good," Lily hummed and stroked him again.

"Jesus," he shouted. He released her and worked his jeans open, giving her more room to slide her hand up his shaft. He kicked his jeans off, leaving his black boxer briefs on. His t-shirt went down on her next stroke.

Lily couldn't decide where to put her hands. She was getting wetter by the second with her hand wrapped around his cock, but his chest was too sexy to resist.

Archer pulled her hand from his boxer briefs so he could strip her clothes off her. Her shirt went first, then his hands cupped her breasts and teased her nipples through the cotton of her bra.

"Oh, God," Lily murmured.

He added his mouth, using his teeth just enough to feel through the fabric, and she nearly shot off just that fast.

"Don't hold back with me, Lily. I want to hear and feel all of you. Give it all to me."

Lily helped him get her pants off and took her panties with them. She was so wet she practically dripped, and he hadn't even touched her yet.

Archer kissed and sucked her nipples, but Lily needed

more. She slid one hand between them and down to her clit. One swipe over the sensitive flesh and she gasped.

"Are you gonna make yourself come, Lily?"

"Yes," she whispered.

"Show me how you like to be touched, beautiful. Lay down for me and let me watch you."

She'd never masturbated in front of anyone else. It felt way too personal to share with a guy she'd only met a day ago, but the heat in his eyes and the gravely tone of his voice said he was as turned on as she was.

She stretched out on her bed and spread her thighs. He took his boxer briefs off, distracting her from her goal. He was impossibly long, his rigid cock standing straight up. Dark hair went from his nipples in a vee straight to his beautiful dick. She wanted it in her mouth.

She licked her lips, eyes focused on him. He wrapped a hand around it, and her heart kicked up a beat.

"Watch me while I watch you."

Lily let her hand fall to the apex of her thighs as Archer stroked himself. She gathered moisture from her center and spread it up to her clit. Archer watched her, his gaze focused intently on where her hand was.

She started off slow, her self-consciousness telling her he didn't really want to watch her come. Her gaze flipped between his face and his cock, watching him for clues that she should stop.

"Are you trying to torture me?" he growled. "You came faster than this the other night. I might not be able to wait for you."

"Is this turning you on?"

He met her eyes and nodded. Just once. It was all he could do. The muscles in his neck were corded tight, his shoulders tense. His forearms looked twice their normal size. His breath came in shallow pants, like he'd run a few miles instead of standing in a bedroom.

"Lily," he said, all the desperation and desire pouring out of him in that one little word.

She couldn't hold back anymore. Her fingers flew over her clit, vibrating over just the top until she was panting as hard as he was. She set one finger right on her clit and pressed harder as she moved her hand. Her hips lifted off the bed, her orgasm tearing through her so hard and fast she couldn't breathe.

"Oh, fuck, Lily," Archer groaned. "Fuck, make that pussy come."

She came again, harder, at the deep sound of his voice.

"Jesus, I'm gonna come," he panted.

"Inside me. Please, Archer."

"Condom."

"Nightstand."

She dug it out and helped him roll it on. As soon as she was on her back again, he thrust into her, so deep and hard that she came a third time.

"Oh, fuck," he whispered, stilling inside her as she rode out her orgasm.

"Sorry," she panted. "Oh, God, that was good."

"We're not done yet, sweetheart. We have all night."

12

———

ARCHER WANTED TO CLAW HIS THROAT OUT. HE NEEDED TO come so badly he felt like he was going to vomit. But nothing was going to stop him from fucking Lily until she couldn't speak.

Watching her touch herself was the single most erotic experience of his life. She was amazing. He'd lived with all men for long enough that he'd been walked in on more than once, and seen too many dicks for his sanity, but watching a woman pleasure herself, one who was doing it for her own benefit and not that of whatever camera was trained on her, was seriously fucking hot.

When Lily's body stopped pulsing around him, he finally choked back the pain of holding back his own pleasure and was able to focus on her again. She likes it fast and rough, he could tell that, but she also liked to be touched and kissed. She had a thing for her nipples, and she was sensitive. Archer was going to make damn good use of the recon he'd done.

He eased out of her body and slid back in slowly. She

whimpered but didn't protest. He did it again, tugging a cup down on her bra when he moved. He kept up his slow pace in and out of her and tasted her sweet flesh.

She moaned and held his head in place, her sexy body writhing beneath him as he tortured them both with his slow pace.

He switched to the other breast, moving that cup aside, and laved and nipped at her until she moaned for him to make her come.

"You're still talking so I haven't done my job yet," Archer teased.

"Nope, you definitely haven't," Lily panted. "I haven't come anywhere near enough tonight. Although I've tripled the number of orgasms I've had with another person in the last year, so there is that."

Archer growled and thrust hard into her. She gasped and her body arched toward his. "No talking about other men when I'm inside you."

She giggled. "Sorry. You're much better than he was. And bigger. Huge."

Archer glared at her. "See, now I don't believe you."

She giggled again and shook her head. "Trust me. The only reason I had an orgasm with him was because he got lucky."

"If he was with you, he was damn lucky."

She smiled. "You're sweet."

"And you're sexy as hell. Now, no more talking about men with tiny dicks."

She started to laugh, then moaned when he thrust hard into her.

"You feel so good," she whispered. "Before the end of the night, I need you in my mouth."

"Oh, fuck," Archer groaned, thrusting harder. "Are you serious?"

Lily nodded. "Yeah. Your cock is beautiful. I want to taste it."

"Jesus," Archer growled. "Fuck, Lily. I love your dirty mouth."

"Oh, yeah? Then I bet you're gonna love knowing that I'm going to lick your cock, run my tongue from one end to another. Then I'll wrap my lips around it and suck hard on you. I know you're bigger than I can handle, so I'll use my hand to stroke you while I suck you as deep as I can get you."

He groaned and pumped harder and faster into her as she tortured him with her words.

"When you think you're going to come, I'm going to tease your balls and make sure you come so hard your eyes roll back in your head. I want to feel your come hit the back of my throat."

"Fuck. Lily, I'm gonna come. Are you close?"

She shook her head. "No. But I'm good."

"Oh, shit," Archer yelled. He wanted to wait for her, but he couldn't stop the flow. His spine ached from holding back. His release exploded through him and brought a yell loud enough to rattle the windows in the old building with it.

He collapsed on top of Lily, his muscles aching. He didn't even have the strength to roll them over so he wasn't crushing her.

"Sorry. Move... in... minute."

She wrapped her arms and legs around him and shook her head. "I like feeling your weight on top of me. Makes me feel safe."

He pushed up to look at her. "I'm not going to let anything happen to you, Lily."

She nodded. "I know."

Archer kissed her softly and realized it was the first time he'd kissed her since before he stripped her. "I should have kissed you more."

She laughed. "That's what you're thinking about right now?"

He nodded. "I should have romanced you or something. Anything instead of jerking off in front of you and telling you I want you."

Lily sobered. "This was exactly what I needed and exactly what I wanted. I'm not a romance kind of girl. I prefer reality. And reality is that romance is dead and men are usually only good for two things."

"What are those?"

"Reaching things down from high shelves and opening jars."

Archer's eyebrows shot up. "Really? Sex doesn't even make the list?"

Lily shrugged nonchalantly. "It's been almost a year since I've had sex. I kind of learned it's not that big of a deal. Not when you have really good vibrators."

Archer rolled back on top of her. "I'm going to have to show you a few things a vibrator can't do." He slid down the bed until he was eye-level with her beautiful pussy. She smelled like heaven, a musky scent that made him feel drunk.

Lily watched him with interest. Right up until he swiped his tongue through her folds. Then her eyes rolled back in her head, and he set about proving to her men were good for orgasms, too.

Really, really good.

ARCHER WOKE up early the next morning, long before the sun. Lily was on her side, facing away from him and snoring softly. He grabbed his jeans and pulled them on before he snuck out of the room, closing the door quietly behind himself.

"Walk of shame?" Jack said from the darkness.

Archer flipped off the lump on the couch.

"Sounded like a hell of a night. You wear her out?"

"None of your fucking business."

Jack snorted. "When I'm subjected to it all night, it kind of is. Didn't see her as your type."

Archer spun on his friend, pissed off and ready to defend Lily. "Why the fuck not?"

The couch rustled as Jack sat up. "She's way too nice for you. She's the kind of woman a guy wants to bring home to his mother, not do the kinds of things you normally do to one."

"I like nice. Why can't I like nice?"

Jack stared at him in the darkness for far too long. Archer wanted him to spill it already, but Jack was a sniper. They were known for their patience.

Just when Archer was about to give up and get some coffee, Jack spoke.

"We're not made for a woman like her. She's sweet and naive. She doesn't need your shit in her world."

"You mean Rodney?"

Jack shook his head. "I mean all of it. I know the shit you've done. I've seen the shit you've seen. None of it is easy to swallow, and guys like us? We're not meant for forever."

"Who said anything about forever?"

"Maybe no one, but do they ever? Usually it comes out of

fucking nowhere and is a two-by-four on the side of the head."

"Speaking from experience?" Archer joked.

Jack was silent a moment too long. "Yeah, Hulk. I am. I've been where you are. Sleeping with a woman who told me she wasn't looking to get attached. I thought she was someone I could have fun with, but I was wrong."

"What happened?" Archer had to know.

"She killed herself when I told her we were over and I wasn't coming back."

"Fuck."

"I know you think Lily is someone you can have fun with, but there are shadows in her eyes. She's seen pain, too. Be careful with her."

Archer nodded once, annoyed that Jack picked up on something he missed. It wasn't fair that he was jealous of Jack's perception where Lily was concerned, but he was. He didn't want to think about any other man knowing anything about her that he didn't know.

Jack laid back down, and Archer went into the kitchen. He fixed coffee in the dark and took his mug out to the patio off the living room. The bite of the cool morning air helped remind Archer he was back in the good ol' US of A instead of the wasteland he spent the better half of his last dozen years. He sipped his black coffee and watched the sun lift over the trees instead of blend into the endless sand of the desert.

It was good to be home.

Archer snorted. He never thought he'd say that about being in Niagara Falls. He escaped as quickly as he could when he was younger, running to the opposite coast so he could be a SEAL. He loved every minute of his career, even the training that he thought would kill him some days.

But he was back to square one. His military experience didn't lend well to civilian life. He didn't have a degree to fall back on. He could go back to school, but he was never very good at taking tests and the idea of spending the next four years, at least, in college with kids almost half his age did not sit well.

Which left Archer with zero options and even fewer ideas.

The door slid open behind him, and Jack walked out with his own cup of coffee. They stood and watched the quiet morning in silence for a few minutes.

"I know it's not my business. I'm sorry," Jack said finally.

Archer shook his head. "It's fine. I appreciate the thought. And I'm sorry about your ex. It's a shit thing to do, then to blame you for it. I can't see Lily doing anything like that."

Jack shook his head. "Neither can I, but I didn't expect Meredith to do it either."

"How long were you with her?" Archer asked, leaning against the railing.

Jack shrugged. "Not long. A couple months before I deployed one time. She was a local."

"How did you meet?"

Jack huffed a laugh. "I really don't want to talk about my dead ex. Isn't there anything else we can talk about?"

Archer laughed. "Yeah, sorry. How was your trip home?"

Jack snorted. "You really know how to pick shitty topics."

"Why? What happened?"

"My dad wants me home to run the family business. My mom wants me home because why would I go anywhere else."

"What do you want?"

Jack shrugged. "I don't know. I never thought I'd feel this

lost after we left. I hated growing up on a soybean farm, and have no plans to go back there, but I don't know where I want to be. I know this sucks for you, but being together and looking for your brother is the most I've felt like myself since we walked."

Archer nodded. "I know what you mean."

They sat on the patio in silence and watched the apartment complex come to life around them. Archer hadn't had a chance to just sit and do nothing in forever. Forget about Jaymes and Lily and his future. Just enjoy existing.

The door slid open again, and Lily walked out. She smiled at both of them and leaned against the railing between them. "Morning gentlemen."

"Morning, beautiful," Jack said, earning a growl from Archer. Jack laughed.

Archer wanted to pull Lily into his arms and give her a proper good morning, but he wasn't sure how she was feeling. Would she be pissed that he left the bed before she was awake? Was she done with him after one night? Was she afraid to kiss him in front of Jack?

He settled on saying good morning and signaling to Jack to go back inside so he could have a minute with Lily. Thankfully, Jack got the hint and listened to it.

"Hey," Archer said when they were alone.

"Hey. I wondered where you were when I woke up. I'm usually a pretty light sleeper."

Archer rested his hands on either side of her hips, caging her in against the railing. "I hope I wore you out last night."

Lily looked up at him with eyes full of lust. "I'm hoping you do it again tonight."

Archer grinned and nuzzled against her throat, taking his time kissing and nibbling on her skin. She moaned a soft, throaty sound that went straight to his cock. He leaned into her, letting her feel what she did to him.

"Why don't I have today off so I can just drag you back to my bed and have my way with you all day?" she whined.

It took a few seconds for her words to sink into Archer's consciousness, but when they did, he drew back. "What do you mean? You're not going to work."

Lily flinched. "Of course I am. Why wouldn't I?"

"Did you miss the note on your fridge about someone taking you if we didn't stop looking for Jaymes?"

Lily huffed. "I saw it. And trust me, I remember it. But I don't know what that has to do with me not being allowed to go to work."

"We can't watch you if you're at work. You have to call in."

Lily laughed for a second, then stopped suddenly. "You're serious, aren't you?"

Archer nodded. "Absolutely. You need to be here where I can keep my eyes on you at all times."

"I'm pretty sure you got more than an eyeful last night," she taunted, pressing her curves to his body again.

It had her desired effect and made him lose track of what they were talking about as he dove for her lips, sealing his to hers and getting lost in her. He took what he needed from her, devouring her. He let her make him forget about everything that plagued him. Her, his brother, his future. He could stay lost in her forever.

Whoa. Forever? Archer wasn't a forever kind of guy. He was an everything's temporary guy.

No. Forever was just saying he wasn't sick of her yet. But he had an obligation to keep her safe. Which meant she couldn't go to work.

"Can't go to work," he murmured against her throat as he kissed his way down it again. "Stay here."

She laughed. "I think the only way you'd convince me was if you were going to be in my bed all day distracting me. I can't sit around here again and worry about Jaymes. I know you're here and you're going to find him. I need to work. To feel normal. There are people counting on me."

Archer took a step back to clear his head. She made him want to lock her in a room and block out the rest of the world. He hated the thought of anything happening to her, and she was so cavalier about it. Like she was indestructible simply because she had a job. He had a job, too. And his was to make sure she didn't vanish.

"What is more important than your safety?"

"I'll be safe at work. I won't go anywhere alone, and I'll be surrounded by people all the time. I always am. There's no reason to worry."

"I'm not worried," Archer scoffed.

Lily grinned and sidled up to him. "I can see it in your eyes. You're worried about me. It's sweet."

"I'm not sweet."

Lilly patted his chest. "I know you think that, but you are. Trust me, that's not a bad thing. Every woman wants some sweet at the end of the day. It's why I bake so much, and have the ass to prove it."

Archer cupped her ass and pulled her against him. "This is a perfect ass. Those sweet things you have at the end of the day are well worth it if it makes you happy. You're sexy as fuck, Lily."

She moaned and pressed against him. "You make me forget about all the things I should be doing."

"Forget about them and stay here. You'll be safer."

She chuckled and shook her head, ducking her chin.

"You'll be trying to find Jaymes. You and the rest of your Team. I'll just be in the way. I'll leave you guys some good menus and I promise I'll cook dinner tonight, but I really need to go to work."

Archer sighed. "Fine, but I'm dropping you off and picking you up."

Lily smiled. "I can handle that."

13

———————

LILY TRIED TO CONVINCE HERSELF NOTHING WAS OUT OF THE ordinary, but she was paranoid. Every time she stepped on an elevator, she looked for menacing people. She heated up her lunch and nearly screamed when it popped. She even freaked out when one of her coworkers walked into her office with a question.

"Are you okay?" Adam asked, eyes narrowed.

Lily nodded. "Sorry. I wasn't expecting you to be there."

He tilted his head, dark hair falling over his shoulder. His brown eyes always seemed kind to Lily, but as she watched him, she wondered if they were calculating behind his nice-guy look.

"I knocked."

Lily smiled. "I know. Sorry. I was just lost in what I'm doing. What's up?"

"Don't get too lost or we might never find you again," Adam teased.

"What do you mean by that?" Lily demanded, her spine tingling with fear. They were alone in her office. Sure, she could scream if he tried to kidnap her, but if he had a gun, what would she do? She should have asked Archer for some self-defense moves she could use on an armed assailant.

Adam grinned. "Just don't want to lose you. You always seem to know the answers. Bobby never helps me when I have questions, but you do. You really should be our boss instead of him."

Lily relaxed fractionally. "Thanks. Um, so, what did you need?"

He held up a tablet. "Right. I was working on opening up more access to the patients. Giving them access to the test results, like we talked about. The problem is every time I do it, I end up giving them access to everything. There has to be a permission that I'm not assigning right. I was hoping you could look at it with me."

Lily motioned for him to bring the tablet over and sit next to her. He handed over the device and showed her the two screens he had.

They spent the next couple of hours looking at what he was working on until they figured it out together.

"That seems so easy now. Thanks, Lily."

"Any time."

Adam grinned. "Hey, uh, I was wondering if you're doing anything this weekend. Maybe we could grab dinner?"

Panic welled up in her chest. She hated dating coworkers. It either ended badly and was awkward, or it was just bad. Turning them down wasn't any better. She didn't have much experience with either, which made it that much worse.

The phone on her desk rang, breaking her trance and giving her an excuse to put Adam off. "Sorry, I really need to take this."

He grinned. "No problem. You know where to find me."

She smiled and lifted the receiver as he stepped into the hallway. "Lily Scott."

"Why haven't you been answering your phone?" Archer demanded.

The possessive, scared tone of his voice sent a spark racing up her spine. "I was in a meeting."

"With who?"

"Seriously?"

"Lily, someone kidnapped my brother and threatened to take you. You're damn right I'm serious."

"Adam Hollis. He's a coworker. He needed help with something."

"Search Adam Hollis," Archer said to someone in the background.

"Don't search him. He's harmless."

"No one is harmless, Lily. What did he say?"

"About what? We talked about work."

"Why didn't you check in with me? I told you to call me every two hours or I'd call you. I was about to come there and tear the place apart to find you."

"I told you I'd be safe here." She was *not* going to tell him about her paranoia. It would only make Archer's paranoia worse.

He grunted. "What time do you need me to pick you up?"

Lily glanced at the clock. "I should be done by five-thirty. I'll meet you out front."

"I'll come in and get you."

"Archer."

"No, Lily. Stay inside where other people are. I'll be there at five-thirty."

"Okay." She paused. "Hey Archer?"

"Yeah?"

"Thanks."

He chuckled softly. "Any time, sweetheart."

She hung up with a smile.

"SHE OKAY?" Dunn asked when Archer hung up.

Archer nodded. "In a meeting."

"Feel better?"

Archer glared at his friend and nodded sharply.

"Are you too close to this one?"

"No."

"Jack said you two slept together."

"Hell, no. I wouldn't touch Jack."

Dunn chuckled and shook his head. "You know what I mean. You and Lily."

Archer shrugged and neutralized his expression. He could not be removed from the mission. It was his brother, and the woman he was sleeping with. He wasn't getting benched. "Why does that matter?"

"You can't think clearly when your dick is the one in charge."

"My dick isn't in charge. I am. Always."

Dunn crossed his arms and rocked back on his heels. His dark skin blended into the black of his t-shirt, making it hard to tell what was man and what was fabric. His arms ticked, a sign Dunn was pissed off. He didn't get pissed off easily, but when he did, they all knew to back off.

"I don't think that's the case here, Ford. We're looking for your brother, which makes this whole thing personal. Now you're fucking the woman who called you and got us all here. Do we know for sure that she isn't involved? That she's not a mole pulling the strings?"

"Don't you dare accuse her of that. She's honest and kind and she cares about my brother. She'd never use him like that."

"What about you? Would she use you?"

Archer glared. He hated to admit that he didn't have an answer. Lily could tell him anything, and he had no way to know if it was the truth. She could be sleeping with Jaymes. She could be working with whoever took him. She could be someone else entirely and the real Lily was taken, too. He had no way of knowing.

"Did you check up on her?"

Dunn nodded. "Of course."

"And?"

"She seems legit, but we don't know for sure. The questions are still valid."

Archer ran a hand down his face and sighed. He wasn't the brains or the leader. He wasn't the one who figured things out. He was just there and went in whatever direction he was told to go. With this op, he felt like he had to do it all. Yeah, the team was doing more than their share of the heavy lifting, but they were all looking to him since it was his brother.

And now Lily.

"What should I do?"

Dunn shrugged. "You're not going to like it."

"Like what?"

"When we get a lead, fill her in. If it blows up, we'll go from there."

Archer's mouth was dry, like he swallowed a bag of cotton balls. Testing Lily felt wrong, like he was waiting for her to fuck up. On the other hand, if she was the one who was holding his brother, he had to know.

"Okay."

Dunn nodded, then walked away.

Archer joined the rest of the team in the living room. Everyone was quiet, focused on their part of things. Archer went back to their board. It was far too blank for him. They knew someone took Jaymes, someone was threatening Lily, and it might have something to do with the power plant.

But what?

"Yes!" English yelled from the other room. "Yes, I got it! Hell yeah. Look at this."

Archer went in there as English was spinning his laptop toward the living room to show them a map.

"What is that?"

"I've been working on pinpointing a location for the email Jaymes sent to Lily. It went through a bunch of different servers and bounced around the world, but I finally tracked it to the source. He's here. He's still in Niagara Falls."

Dunn stepped forward. "Okay, but where?"

English grinned, his boyish smile making him look younger than thirty. "Two miles from here. Near the power plant."

"Let's go," Archer demanded, checking his Glock and slipping an extra magazine into his pocket. He reached for his bulletproof vest and had it on before he realized no one else was moving.

"We need a plan, Ford. We can't just bust in there and expect to come out in a good position," Dex said.

Archer didn't care about a plan. It was his brother. He owed him. He wasn't going to let him sit another fucking minute in some hellhole just because they wanted to sit around and swap stories. No. Fuck no.

Dunn stepped up. "Listen, you know he's right. We'll get Jaymes back alive, but we need to do this the right way if that's going to happen. Go pick up Lily from work. We'll set the plan. When you two get back, we'll tell you what we're going to do."

Dunn's message was clear. Get the fuck out and bring the mole back. He'll do the dirty work of telling her everything so he can be the one who slams her when it all falls apart.

That didn't make Archer feel any better.

He finally nodded, removed his vest, and stomped his way to his SUV. He drove like an asshole to the hospital where Lily worked. He was early, which meant he could catch her before she walked outside and into harm's way.

A purple jacket stood out against the sleek metal and glass structure. Archer swore and moved closer, knowing it was Lily before he reached her.

"I told you to stay inside."

"And I told you I was safe here."

"Did anything happen today?"

She shook her head. "Not unless a coworker asking me out is significant."

Archer slid her a look. He did not like the idea of her going out with someone else. She spent the night in *his* arms, calling out *his* name, and she was in *his* truck talking about a date with another guy?

"What did you say?" he growled.

She scoffed. "No, of course."

A whole different kind of panic worked its way up his spine. Did she think they were something they'd never be? Did she say no because they slept together and she was convinced that they were going to live happily ever after?

"Why?"

She snorted. "Because I don't date, and I especially don't date men I work with. Don't worry, I haven't forgotten how things are with us. I didn't dream of white dresses and picket fences last night, or all day today. Just orgasms and you filling me up."

She nipped his ear and suckled her way down his neck. He did his best to focus on the road, but she was distracting him. His cock rose, pressing hard against his zipper. She palmed him through his jeans, and he finally gave in and pulled over.

Wedged just barely between two cars on a street with endless traffic flowing by, Archer yanked the lever to send his seat all the way back and dragged Lily onto his lap at the same time. He left the SUV running, but slammed it in park and made much better use of his hands on her ass.

"So first you're jealous that another guy asked me out, then you're terrified that I said no because of you. You can't have it both ways, Archer Ford."

He slid his hands up her ribcage and cupped her breasts, teasing her nipples through the lace of her bra. "I want you all ways, Lily Scott."

"I've never had sex in a vehicle before," she whispered. "With all these cars going right past us, knowing all they have to do is slow down and they'll know exactly what we're doing."

"You're a bit of an exhibitionist, aren't you?"

She shook her head. "Nope. I'm usually really private. There's something about you that makes me so crazy that I can't stop to think about anything besides getting you inside me."

He thrust up against her and they both moaned. "I'm not so sure your jeans are going to work for sex in the front seat, sweetheart. Should have worn a skirt."

She moaned and whimpered at the same time. "I don't think I can wait until we get home."

"Shit," Archer swore, resting his head against her collarbone. "Shit. I can't believe I forgot."

"Forgot what?" she asked, stroking his hair with one hand.

"English thinks he found where they're keeping Jaymes."

"What?" she gasped, pulling back so fast she slammed into the steering wheel and blasted the horn. "Sorry. They found him? Why are we here?"

She climbed off Archer and settled into her seat quickly. Her seatbelt was back on before Archer had his chair moved forward again. She wasn't acting like a woman who was working with the people who took Jaymes.

Their drive back to the apartment was tense. Lily was silent the whole time, clenching and unclenching her fists and twisting a ring around her index finger. She chewed the inside of her cheek.

Archer catalogued all of it, taking mental notes as he debated with himself if she was anxious about finding Jaymes because she wanted to see him again, or because she didn't want to see him again.

She rushed inside, bounding up the stairs ahead of Archer. He was on her heels when she burst into Jaymes's apartment. "You found him?" she asked.

Everyone in the room looked at Williams. He wasn't the CO, but he was still in charge. He was the guy who answered questions and told them all what to do.

"We think so," Williams said, glancing at Archer.

Archer nodded subtly, knowing Dunn told him everything.

"We're going to go get him. English found where he was when he sent you that email. We have a plan."

She nodded, her shoulders sagging with relief. "Thank you. Thank you so much." She moved to leave the room.

"Don't you want to know what we're doing?" Williams asked.

Lily shook her head. "I wouldn't understand half of it. I'm going to take a shower and relax. Then I'm going to make Jaymes's favorite double chocolate cake. Thank you. All of you."

"We haven't found him yet," Dunn reminded her.

Lily nodded. "I know. But you will. Archer promised me you guys would bring him home. I know you will."

She left them all staring after her.

When the bathroom door closed, Archer glanced at Dunn. "She's not involved."

Dunn shook his head. "It doesn't seem that way."

"Did she take her phone?" Williams asked.

Archer looked through her purse and didn't find it. "Yeah."

"Then she could be calling to tell them we're coming. Let's go. Ford, we'll fill you in on the way, but if we're actually going to find your brother, alive, we need to go now."

Archer nodded. "Hooyah."

14

ARCHER SLID OUT OF THE SECOND SUV SILENTLY AND CLOSED the door behind himself. It was still light out, but where they were was quiet. A few houses dotted the horizon, but it was flat across the cemetery grounds.

The canal stretched out to the south, the direction they were going. English was directing them from Jaymes's apartment through comms they all were tapped into.

Archer didn't speak to Lily before they all left. He listened to his CO and piled into the SUV's so he could find his brother. There would be time to question Lily later. After they found Jaymes.

The trees provided them cover until darkness settled over the area. Archer listened to the instructions being repeated in his ear.

Follow me.

Stay low.

We're civilians now. And this isn't war.

The fuck it wasn't. Someone took his brother. It most definitely *was* war.

Archer moved behind Dunn with Dex. Williams had

Adrian and Slade behind him. Jack hung back, secure in his perch, watching everyone's six.

The empty stretch of grass between the trees and the building Jaymes was believed to be in seemed like it was miles. When Dunn set out to run, Archer put his head down and followed him, bracing himself for the gunshot he knew was coming any second.

They reached the building and pressed against the metal side. The heat from the day still radiated off the surface. Archer couldn't hear anything except his own heart pounding in his ears.

Williams' team rushed into place on the other side of the door after a sweep of the structure to make sure there weren't any other ways out.

"On me," Williams said. "Bravo, stay outside. If they get past us, get 'em."

"Copy," Dunn said quietly enough that Archer only heard him through his earpiece.

"I want to be in there," Archer hissed.

"And that's exactly why you're not going to be. Let them do their job."

Archer listened as Alpha Team worked their way inside the building. It was little more than a bunker with metal walls, an old wooden roof, and a tiny parking lot. English's search revealed that the place was once used for cremation, but the cemetery built a brand new facility years earlier and had all but abandoned the small building on the edge of their property.

A door creaked open slowly, but silence filled Archer's ears after that.

"What's going on?" he whispered.

"Nothing," came the answer. "No one's here. But there's something you need to see."

Archer glanced at Dunn and Dex. Dunn stayed at the door to guard it, nodding for Archer and Dex to go inside.

Archer moved through the dark, dank tunnels. Everything smelled damp and musty. The water wasn't far, and judging by the walls as they worked their way deeper underground, it seeped into everything around the small building.

They reached a door. The shuffle of feet inside told them the other half of the team was there. Archer went in first, pushing the creaky door open with his gun. Dex was right behind him.

"It's us," Williams said. "Look at this."

Archer moved across the room to where Williams pointed. The metallic scent filled his nose before his eyes adjusted to the darkness at the far edge of the room.

"Blood."

Rocky nodded. "Lots of it. Concrete floor didn't absorb much. I'm going to run some tests. Will need some of yours."

Archer nodded. He didn't understand all the medical stuff their former EMT turned SEAL did, but he knew Adrian needed blood to test against what was on the floor to find out if it was a family match to Archer's. It was the only way to tell if it was actually Jaymes.

"What happened?" Archer demanded, spinning to face the others.

Williams ran a hand down his face, smearing the grease paint he put on to hide his light skin. He shook his head. "We don't know. If Johnson is positive this is where they had him, best guess would be someone tipped them off."

"Who could have gotten word to them? We didn't tell anyone what we were doing."

"Lily knew," Dunn said in Archer's ear, all of their ears.

"Fuck you, Pres. Lily didn't do this. We didn't tell her anything."

"Maybe she didn't know the details, but she had plenty of time to make a phone call after she got home from work and warn whoever was here with Jaymes that we were coming."

Archer stared at the pool of blood on the floor. There was no way to know where it came from, but it was a decent amount of blood. He guessed as much as a pint, which meant Jaymes would be hurting. Even more, if the reason it was there was because someone made sure he understood getting messages out wasn't okay.

Archer had a hard time reconciling his idea of Lily with a coldhearted son of a bitch who would kidnap another human being and beat the shit out of them for trying to escape. Sure, he'd been the one in that room before, on both sides, but it took a special kind of fucked up to plan it.

Archer couldn't see Lily doing it.

"You know it's possible," Dunn pushed.

"No, it's not," Archer said. "It's not her. She wouldn't do this. We wouldn't have had that lead if it weren't for her. We wouldn't even be here if she hadn't called me. She has no motive. Fuck, she was threatened."

"What better way to make it look like you're innocent than to be a victim? We've seen it before, and you know it. CI's who turn on us at the last second and we're left with our dicks in our hands. Why would she be any different?"

"All right, gentlemen," Williams said in his booming voice. "This is heated. But it's not getting us anywhere. Dunn, look into Lily. Go through her place tomorrow when she's at work. Again. Archer, dig. Find out what you can. She seems to trust you. The rest of us need to keep looking. If it's not Lily, we need to understand what's going on here. Someone has a plan. And if we don't uncover it and stop it, there's no telling what kind of impact it'll have."

"Yes, sir," they all said in unison.

Rocky tucked the samples he collected into a pocket in his pants and led the way outside. Archer was the last one to leave the small room, imagining his brother sitting at the metal desk in the metal chair. He still saw Jaymes with his arm in a cast when he closed his eyes. He'd have a new shame to add to his list of wrongs where his brother was concerned.

Archer just hoped he'd have his brother to look at again one day.

ALL LILY KNEW WAS that Jaymes wasn't there. She didn't know where there was, and she didn't care. Her best friend was still missing. Liam wasn't talking to her. His brow furrowed as he stared at his computer screen, ignoring her and everything around her.

Even the double chocolate cake she baked that Jaymes wouldn't get to eat.

Lily tried to eat a piece, but the sweet taste turned to cement in her stomach and she had to trash half of it. She was going to be sick. It was all her fault. If she'd called Archer when Jaymes first disappeared, he would be back. But she waited. She convinced herself she was crazy. And her best friend was going to pay for it.

Hell, maybe he already did. Just because he wasn't there didn't mean he was still alive.

The thought of Jaymes being dead was enough to send Lily over the edge. She rushed to the bathroom and kneeled in front of the porcelain throne. She heaved, evicting the cake from her stomach along with everything else she'd eaten that day.

When she finally stopped heaving, Lily flushed the toilet and stood. She splashed cold water on her face and into her mouth. She didn't feel better, but she was on her feet, so that was an improvement.

Yelling drew her attention from the mirror to the apartment on the other side of the door. She opened the door and worked her way toward the living room, stopping dead when she heard her name.

"I can't believe you think Lily did this. How dare you?"

Did what?

"How do you explain that the mark is gone before we show up? Hours before. Early enough that we don't even see them leave. Does that sound like it's a coincidence?" Dunn yelled back.

"Then someone else found out what was happening. Or someone else is the leak. But it's not fucking her! She's not like—"

"Guys!" Jack yelled, getting the attention. He nodded to where Lily stood on the edge of the room, and all eyes swung to her.

Dunn looked away first. Her accuser. The guy who actually thought she kidnapped her best friend. The other guys shuffled their feet, avoiding her, too.

Archer shot daggers at Dunn. Lily was touched by his loyalty to her, even though it was misplaced. He was a SEAL. Loyalty was the thing that made them work. And he was choosing her over Dunn and the rest of the team.

No, she didn't kidnap her best friend, but Archer didn't owe her anything.

"Well, thank you for letting me know what you think, Daniel. Feel free to search my phone, my apartment, my credit cards, everything. Dig as deep as you want to. I didn't kidnap my best friend, you... jerk," Lily said. Her voice shook with her fury and emotions. Tears raced down her cheeks, and she wiped them away ruthlessly. "If you'll excuse me, I'm finding this room a little too full of testosterone at the moment."

Lily held her head high as she walked through the room, stuffed her feet in her sneakers, grabbed her purse, and left. No one said a word, just watched her walk away. She took a shaky breath when she was in the hallway, but she didn't stop. She couldn't stand there and risk one of them opening the door and seeing her collapse.

She rushed down the stairs to her apartment. Before she reached the door, she heard, "Hey, Lily. How's it going?"

"Blake. Um, hi. How are you?" Lily wiped her face, hoping he wouldn't see the tears.

"Are you okay?" he asked, face pinching into a concerned look. "What's wrong?"

Lily shook her head. "Nothing. It's fine."

Blake nodded toward his apartment. "Come inside for a drink. If nothing else, he won't know where you are for a few minutes."

Lily laughed softly and nodded. Blake was a nice guy. Most men ran from a woman when she was crying, but Blake was inviting her inside. After learning Archer's team thought she was the one responsible for the mess they were involved in, she was raw and needed someone to talk to and somewhere to hide.

Blake's apartment was neat, like the other times she'd been there. She'd stopped by once or twice when her mail was delivered to his place and he had to grab it, but she hadn't been there for longer than a few seconds before.

"Take a seat. Let me change real quick and I'll grab us some drinks."

Lily nodded again while Blake disappeared into the

bedroom. His apartment was a reflection of hers with the kitchen to the right and the bedroom to the left. Beyond was his living room with a dark leather couch that looked too inviting for Lily to pass up.

She had to come up with a story for Blake. He was going to ask what was going on, and she had to tell him something. He saw her coming downstairs from Jaymes's apartment when he was coming up the stairs, so Archer was the best excuse. The problem was she couldn't tell Blake much.

She hated wondering if he was involved somehow. She didn't know much about him, but if Daniel could accuse her, she had to wonder who really was guilty.

The idea of it being someone she knew made her dizzy. That someone would target Jaymes to do something that could destroy the power plant, and God knew what else. Archer's team did a background check on Blake, but she had to assume they'd done one on her also.

Hell, she didn't even know what Blake did for a living.

He came back in shorts and a t-shirt that fit him well. She wasn't used to seeing him in casual clothes, looking relaxed and sexy. He was attractive, without question, but he was always just the guy who lived across the hall. Her wounded pride made her see him in a different way. Especially since he rescued her in the hallway.

"What's your poison?" Blake asked, heading to the kitchen.

Lily shrugged. "I'm good with anything right now. As long as it has liquor in it, I'll be happy."

Blake laughed and reached a bottle down from the cabinet above the pass-through, flashing a slice of skin. Lily enjoyed the view, licking her lips and staring at him until he joined her in the living room and handed over a glass.

"Thanks."

"Any time." He sipped. "Do you want to tell me what happened?"

She sighed. "I just got into a fight with Archer and some of his friends."

"Those big military looking guys who've been hanging around lately?"

Lily sipped as she nodded. The liquor was cold from the ice as it slid down her throat. A burn settled in her stomach with the alcohol, radiating through her and bringing her anxiety down just a hair.

"It seems like a lot of guys are up there. What's going on?"

"Just hanging around. They're all fresh out of the Navy and sightseeing a little before they figure out civilians work, too."

Blake laughed. He settled back against the couch and sipped more from his glass.

Lily mimicked his movements, hoping it would make him trust her. Daniel and Archer both told her she couldn't tell anyone what was really going on, so she kept her mouth shut about the truth. Even telling Blake they were military could be too much information, but they already thought she was guilty so what the hell.

"Are they staying in the area?"

Lily shook her head. "No. Archer's the only one from the area, and he doesn't want to be here. He'll leave soon."

"Really? I didn't know Jaymes had a brother, then he shows up here and the two of you are together, but he's going to leave."

"We're not together," Lily refuted immediately.

"No?"

Lily sipped her drink and shook her head.

"He made it pretty clear when I saw the two of you the other day that you were together."

Lily rolled her eyes. "He's possessive. And I don't know why he did that. We hadn't even slept together when he did that." She realized what she admitted and her cheeks warmed. "Sorry. You didn't need to know that."

Blake shook his head. "It's okay. I like knowing things about you, Lily. I've been trying to get your attention for a while, but Jaymes was always around. I thought you two were together."

Lily huffed a laugh. "Everyone seems to think that, but no. He's been my best friend for years, but we've never been anything other than friends."

"And things are over with Archer? It was just a couple days ago that he showed up, and you've met him, slept with him, and are done with him?"

Lily sighed and shook her head. "He's done with me. And that's okay. I'm not a forever kind of girl. It's better that things are over with Archer and me now instead of later. Later is always worse."

Blake shifted closer to her and picked up a strand of her hair. He ran it through his fingers, brushing his knuckles against her throat. "So you're available again?"

She swallowed roughly and nodded. Did she want Blake? His fingers against her skin didn't turn her on the same way Archer's touch did, but things were over with Archer. She'd gone a long time without needing a man, but it was hard to let go of one who affected her the way Archer did. Maybe sleeping with Blake was the way to do it.

Blake leaned in and pressed his lips to her throat. His scruff tickled her neck. She tilted her head back to give him better access and closed her eyes. If she pretended, he could be Archer. If she didn't think, she could even hear Archer's voice. Calling her.

15

———

Where was she? Archer was freaking out. Lily was gone. Rocky wouldn't let him leave until he drew some blood so he could compare it to the sample they took from the bunker they thought Jaymes was in. As soon as the needle was out, Archer was gone.

And so was Lily.

She didn't answer her door when he knocked, so he picked the lock and let himself in. Her apartment was empty.

Panic flooded him and only got worse when he looked outside and saw her red Civic was still in the lot. She was gone, and she hadn't left on her own.

He turned to run back upstairs when the door to the apartment across the hall opened. He nearly fell to his knees and wept when he saw her standing there, looking at him like he was losing his mind.

"What the hell are you doing?" she demanded.

"Looking for you. What are you doing in there?"

Blake, the neighbor Archer met the day he arrived,

appeared behind Lily. He nuzzled against her neck and slid an arm around her waist. "You okay, Lil?"

Archer growled. He saw fucking red. He was going to pummel that son of a bitch for touching his woman. No one was allowed to put a hand on Lily unless he said so.

"Get your hand off her."

Blake looked up at Archer with a challenge in his eyes and a smirk on his lips. "I think Lily's the only one who can tell me that. And considering she just ran away from you, there's no way in hell I'm letting her leave unless I know she's okay."

Archer glared at the stupid fucker who was about three seconds from getting his hand shattered. Archer knew six ways to break a man's hand with only two fingers, and he was more than happy to demonstrate them all for Blake.

Archer stepped forward, ready to take the sonofabitch out, but Lily stopped him with a hand on his chest. Archer looked down at her palm, holding him back from attacking the fucker who had his Goddamn hand on her. She was protecting him?

"Archer, stop. Blake saw me come down here and invited me in when he saw I was upset. You are not allowed to act like either of us did anything wrong."

"I defended you. I was not on their side in this. You know it."

Lily nodded. "I heard what you said, but they're your brothers. You can't choose me over them."

"The fuck I can't. I already did."

Lily tilted her head to the side and shook it. She was so beautiful and so sweet. Dunn was right. He didn't deserve her, even the worst parts of her, if there were any bad parts. But he wanted her. For as long as she wanted him, he had to be in her life. He had to do anything he could to have her by his side.

And if that meant turning his back on the men who'd saved his life more times and in more ways than he could count, he'd do exactly that.

"Lily."

She smiled softly at him. Then she turned to face Blake. "Thank you for the drink. And the talk. I'll see you soon."

Blake kept his hand on her and pulled her close for a hug. His eyes met Archer's over the top of Lily's head. The asshole wasn't done. As soon as Archer turned his back, Blake was going for Lily again.

Which meant one thing. Archer couldn't leave.

LILY WALKED into the apartment ahead of him and went straight to the kitchen. She opened her fridge and poured a glass of water, then leaned against the counter and drank it, ignoring him the entire time.

When she finished her water, she left the kitchen and went to her bedroom. Archer didn't know what the hell to do. He wanted to talk to her, to tell her what happened in that bunker. To talk things out with her. To explain Dunn's words. But he was getting a firm fuck-off vibe from her. She wanted him to go back to his so-called friends and choose them instead of her.

Not a chance in hell.

Archer sat on her couch and leaned back. He closed his eyes, pinching the bridge of his nose.

Where did they go so wrong?

He knew in his gut that the blood was Jaymes's. There was more going on than he could figure out. He was too close and not close enough at the same time. It frustrated the hell out of him to feel something out there but not be able to pinpoint what it was.

The soft shuffle of her feet drew his attention. Archer lifted his head and looked at her. She'd changed into fleece pajama pants and a sweatshirt. Pink fuzzy slippers only added to how cute she was. But the narrowed eyes and crossed arms told him she didn't want to hear that.

"Why did you follow me down here?" she demanded.

Archer sighed. "I know you're not feeding anyone information."

"How do you know that? I could be exactly who Daniel says I am."

He tilted his head to the side. "Are you?"

She shrugged and captured her lip in her teeth.

He was off the couch and dragged her into his arms before the first tear slid off her lashes. He guided her to the couch and settled her on his lap. She fought him, but he wouldn't let her go.

He held her while she cried, just like he did the day he met her. He stroked her hair and pressed his nose against her neck, whispering what he hoped were calming words into her ear.

She wiggled on his lap and his cock figured out what was going on. He kept one hand on her hip to still her, but she moved every few seconds, stirring him to a painful erection that wasn't going away any time soon.

Her wiggling became rhythmic, and he realized what she was doing.

"Lily?"

"I know you don't want me anymore. All the emotions—"

"Don't want you? What the hell are you talking about?"

She tried to push off his lap, but he held tightly to her. "You don't trust me either. You aren't sure. And you don't want to be with someone you don't trust."

He laughed softly, jostling them both. "Dunn made a convincing argument, but he doesn't know you."

"And you do?"

Archer held her eyes and nodded. If there was ever a moment for him to be honest, that was it. He sensed his future depended on the next few seconds. That he was destined to relive them forever, whether the outcome was good or bad.

"It's only been three days, Lil, but I know you. I know you cook because you like to take care of everyone around you, and because it keeps your mind busy. I know you care about the people in your life more than you care about yourself. I know you'd do anything for my brother because he's been there for you when no one else was. I know you're the sweetest, kindest, most amazing woman I've ever met. And most importantly right now, I know you would never do anything to jeopardize another person, especially my brother. You love him too much to risk hurting him. You're not a criminal mastermind."

She shook her head. "I'm not. But if your team thinks all this is my fault, why would they stay here? Why would they help?"

"Because we might be dumb fucks, but we're good at our job," Jack said from the door. "I'm sorry, Lily."

Lily tried to scramble off his lap, but Archer held her still. He wasn't letting her out of his reach until he knew for sure that Jack was there as a friend and not as an informant. Maybe not even then.

"What are you doing here?"

Jack shrugged. "I was hoping to get some sleep."

"Do you believe Dunn?"

Jack flicked his eyes to Lily, then shook his head. Archer appreciated the concern Jack showed for his woman. Lily didn't need to feel like she was being watched in her own home.

"I didn't do anything," Lily whimpered, her whole body trembling.

Jack nodded. "I know. I think Dunn knows, too. He doesn't like not being able to figure things out. It would be an easy call if it was someone close to him, but things aren't always that easy."

"This isn't fucking war," Archer spat.

Jack sucked in a breath. "It's not. But we're all still getting used to the idea of shitty things happening to good people who didn't do anything to deserve them. Over there, it's a different world. Everyone is fighting to survive. Here, we're going about our lives. That doesn't mean everyone is bad."

"We're still at zero."

"Yeah."

"Are there any ideas?"

Jack laughed mirthlessly and shook his head. "They wouldn't talk with me in the room."

Archer closed his eyes. "They think you're going to tell Lily and she's going to tell whoever is holding Jaymes. That's fucking insane."

Jack shrugged. "It'll clear her name. If she doesn't know anything, she can't be accused of warning anyone."

"I didn't know anything last time," Lily yelled.

"You knew we were leaving," Jack explained. "That was enough. It didn't matter where we were going, we had a lead. And you had the opportunity to make a phone call to get whoever was there to clear out."

"I didn't do it!"

Archer stroked her cheek and tried to calm her down, but she was done. She broke the hold he had on her and pushed to her feet. She paced her living room, her eyes not focusing on anything for longer than a second, including him.

"Why would I have called you if I was the one who took him? You never would have known. You don't talk to Jaymes! He joined the fucking Navy for four years and you didn't even know. How would you have found out he was missing if I didn't call you?"

"I know," Archer said, pushing to his feet. He blocked her path, setting his hands on her arms to get her to stop pacing. "I know. If they think about it, they all know, too. Dunn got screwed by an informant—"

"Literally," Jack muttered.

Archer flashed him a glare, then returned his focus to Lily. "He doesn't trust anyone, especially women. He can't see how anything could have gotten out if you didn't share it."

"Well, maybe Jaymes's apartment is bugged. Or maybe someone else is helping to pull the strings."

Archer shook his head. "We swept for bugs. And it's definitely not someone else on the team. Every single one of those guys is someone I'd trust with my life. They'd never do this."

"Agreed," Jack said firmly.

"Then how did someone find out you guys found Jaymes?"

Archer shook his head. "I wish I knew."

"THAT WAS TOO FUCKING CLOSE," he said when he walked into the room. It was a newer site, but still dark and dank. Musty with the hint of mold and gunpowder. They were off the grid this time. Far off the grid. It made things harder, but it was the only way. They couldn't come that close again.

"We got him out in time," the taller guy, Oscar he thought, said.

"Barely. It was too close."

"How were we supposed to know he got an email off to the chick?"

"You were supposed to be watching him," he growled, moving into the guy's space. Oscar was big, but he was bigger. He had years of experience and knowledge on the idiot who was nothing more than a hired gun. You definitely got what you paid for.

"We got him across the border. They won't get him here."

He rolled his eyes. "You're too fucking cocky. They won't give up searching. Not until they find him. Is he almost done with the program?"

Oscar shrugged. "Dunno."

He wanted to put a bullet through the fucker's face right then, but he knew better. He still needed the guy. He was the one with the connection at the border. The guy who could make the whole process easier. It was bad enough they had to sneak back and forth to get everything they needed, but with a hostage, they were running real risks. If they ended up screwed by their contact, all of them would have their asses in a sling.

And he wasn't going down like that.

He walked past the lump of muscle and into the back room where Jaymes sat hovered over his laptop. One cord came out of the wall to bring power to the machine, but that was it. Even if there was wi-fi in the area, he wouldn't be able to get it through the concrete walls and ten feet of dirt above his spot.

"Your twenty-four hours are almost up."

Jaymes met his eyes. The mask concealed his identity, but he still resisted the urge to hide his eyes. The last thing he needed was this guy getting away and having any suspicions about who he was.

The long gash above his eyebrow was held together with tape. The dried blood on his nose said that wasn't his only wound. Oscar and the other guy must have given him shit for them having to move.

Maybe they were worth a little more than he gave them credit for.

"I can't work in these conditions. What was wrong with the last place?"

"Too close to your brother."

Jaymes snorted. "You must have been drinking. My brother isn't anywhere near here."

"Except your girlfriend called him. He's fit pretty seamlessly into your life and her pants from what I can see. They went at it like rabbits all night last night."

Jaymes glared at him. The barb definitely hit the mark.

He laughed. He figured the kid was in love with her, and being able to tell him his brother beat him to the punch was just the icing on the shit sandwich he had for the kid.

"You're lying."

He snorted. "I'll bring you the recording next time I stop by. She's a screamer that one. Damn. She's got a mouth on her that'll make a priest want a piece."

"Fuck you!" Jaymes yelled, jerking up from his seat so fast the chair flipped over behind him and clattered on the ground.

He smiled. "You might want to watch your mouth with me. You know I can get to her. It'll be easy, too. Especially with someone she trusts on my side."

Jaymes paled, and he reached for the surface his computer rested on. "Who?"

He shook his head and clucked. "Now, now, I can't tell you everything. You need to do something for me. That program."

"It's almost done," Jaymes said quietly.

He recognized a beaten man. One who knew he had no more options if he wanted to live. Jaymes was smart, but not smart enough.

"How long?"

"I need another day. I can't see in here. The lighting sucks."

"I'll see about getting you a lamp."

Jaymes nodded sharply.

He smiled and said, "See you tomorrow, Mr. Ford. Get a good night's sleep. I know your brother won't."

He laughed as Jaymes growled behind him. Torturing him was more fun than he expected.

The stocky one walked in with bags of food as he closed the door on Jaymes.

"Can we feed him?"

"You better. If he passes out and doesn't finish his work, I don't need either of you."

They exchanged a look loaded with anger and distrust. They trusted each other, but they didn't trust him. He understood. He didn't blame them. In another situation, they might have been good men to have on his side. But in the one they were in, it was every man for himself.

Which meant he had bullets ready for both of them when the whole thing was over.

16

———

IT WAS AFTER MIDNIGHT BY THE TIME LILY, ARCHER, AND JACK stopped rehashing everything that happened with Jaymes. She didn't feel any closer to figuring out who was behind the whole thing. The only thing she knew was it wasn't her.

Thankfully, Archer and Jack believed her, but they didn't have any suggestions who else it could be.

"Let's go to bed," Archer said.

"I want to figure this out," Lily argued.

Archer stood and dragged her to her feet. "We'll look again tomorrow. We need some sleep."

Jack snorted.

"Stuff it."

Jack threw his hands up and shook his head. "I didn't say a word."

"You said enough," Archer argued. He wrapped an arm around Lily and guided her away from their notes and toward her bedroom.

The closer they got, the more tired she felt. She was emotionally drained on top of exhausted. She went through the motions of brushing her teeth and changing into her pajamas, but as soon as she crawled under her covers and wrapped herself in Archer's arms, she got a second wind.

"We'll figure this out," he whispered against her hair.

"I don't want to think about it anymore."

"Really?" he asked, pulling back slightly. "You're tense. Like you're still thinking about it all."

"I'm tense, but it has nothing to do with Jaymes."

"Then what..." He laughed softly and nuzzled against her. "Really?"

She shrugged and snuggled even closer to him. His cock hardened between them, pressing into her belly. "I think you're having the same problem I am."

"What? That it's been entirely too long since I was inside you?"

Lily nodded, biting her lip. "Are you sure you trust me?"

Archer tilted her chin up so she had no choice but to meet his eyes in the darkened room. With the door closed, the only hints of light came from her power strip and slivers of moonlight peeking through her blinds. His breath, warm and minty, fanned over her cheeks. His skin was hot and smooth under her fingers. She couldn't get enough of the man who would leave her as soon as he found her best friend.

"I trust you. Absolutely."

She sucked in a shaky breath, her chest expanding and pressing tighter to his. "Thank you."

He kissed her gently on the nose. His lips lingered a little too long, then moved to her eyelids. From there, they went to her cheeks and finally to her lips.

She sighed into him, letting him take over all her sensations. Lily was never particularly forceful in bed, but she always held on to some level of control. She didn't like feeling like any man had a say in how she felt, even when he was making her feel good. But with Archer, she let down all her barriers. The ones she held in place the night before crumbled when he defended her. When he was willing to walk away from his team in order to defend her. She'd never had a man choose her over anyone else, and while she hated that he had to, it made her feel cared for in a way she'd never known.

She wouldn't say *loved* because she knew Archer didn't love her. They'd only known each other a couple of days. Love wasn't possible in that short of a time. Lily certainly didn't love him. He was just really good in bed. And nice to look at. And protective. And kind. And funny. And a damn good kisser. And an incredible person. And…

Shit, maybe she *was* starting to fall for him.

Before Lily got too far down that train of thought, Archer eased her tank top over her head and lowered his lips to her nipples. She arched into him, pressing her over-sized breasts into his mouth. He moaned and moved over her, his large body settling on top of hers.

She closed her eyes and stopped thinking. Thinking could be done when he was asleep and she could freak out alone. She wanted to feel him. To lose herself in him.

She rubbed the back of his head, the sharp prickles of his hair bristling on her fingertips. His erection dug into her thigh. His one hand supported her breast, keeping it right where he wanted it as he devoured her.

He switched sides and repeated the process on the other one, leaving her in a puddle of need by the time he moved lower.

Lower. Wait, lower?

"Archer?"

"You showed me yesterday how you like to come. Now I get to show you how I like to make a woman come."

"So didn't need to hear that right now," she groaned. "If I'm not allowed to talk about other men, you can't talk about other women."

He kissed below her belly button and nipped at her sensitive skin. "You're the only one I'm thinking about coming right now, Lily. I can't wait to taste you. To listen to you. To feel you. Will you let me?"

Well, when he put it like that, how could she say no?

She nodded and chewed her lip. For her, it was the ultimate trust. Few men had given her orgasms, but she hadn't let anyone even try with his mouth since she was in college and the guy she was seeing failed miserably to come close. She ended up waiting until he went back to his dorm, then finishing herself off.

It was after that relationship ended that she decided men were only sometimes worth the orgasm. If they could even get her there.

Archer slid her panties and shorts down her legs, kicking the covers off her bed as he moved with her clothes. When they were free of her legs, he kneeled on the bed and looked at her.

She knew he couldn't see much, but she closed her eyes anyway. She didn't want to watch his erection fade or his gaze skip over the flabby parts that showed how much she loved baking.

"Damn, you're beautiful."

She chuckled. "Yeah, okay. If I lost a bunch of weight maybe."

Archer slid his hands up her thighs. "No. You. Are. Beautiful. Just as you are, Lily. I'm a sucker for a curvy woman, and you're—"

"The curviest one you've ever seen?" she supplied with a laugh.

He crawled up the bed, keeping his body off hers as he moved closer. He hovered over her until he was nose to nose with her. He slowly lowered his body onto hers, letting her feel his weight, starting from his chest. "Even if you were, and you're not, you're the sexiest woman I've ever seen."

When his cock notched between her thighs, she gasped. He was hard, rigid even. He didn't move as he pressed into the gap she made for him, not entering her, just letting her feel how badly he wanted her. How hard he was for her.

"I wouldn't be here right now if I didn't want to be. I wouldn't have threatened Jack that I'd break his fingers if he touched you. I wouldn't have turned my back on my team. I did all of that for you. Because of you. Because I want you. I trust you. I want to be here with you. So don't tell me you're not perfect because in my eyes, you absolutely are."

He brushed the hair back from her face and held her gaze. She nibbled her lip and whispered, "Thank you."

"Now that we got that out of the way, I'm going to go back to my original plan."

He was gone in the next breath, wedging his broad shoulders between her thighs and spearing his tongue into her.

She didn't have time to prepare for how it would feel. Her hips jerked off the bed, burying him in her core. He moaned and did it again and again until she was too far gone to control her movements.

He slid his tongue up until he circled her clit, and her hips jerked again. "Oh, God. Archer, please. I need to come so bad."

He thrust two fingers into her and drew her clit between his teeth, sending her off on a rocket instantly. She moaned and thrashed and grabbed his head and held him against her. He pressed his fingers to her secret spot, and she fell back to the bed, limp while her orgasm controlled the twitches and tremors that wracked her body.

He withdrew from her and dragged his lips up her body until he was nose to nose with her. She smelled her own tangy flavor on him. He kissed her cheek, but she pulled him to her lips. She needed to kiss him.

She thrust her tongue between his lips, tasting herself on him. The mixture of her come and his masculine flavor messed with her head, making her greedy for more of him. She wrapped her legs around his back and drew him closer.

He cupped her hips and drove into her. They both pulled back from their kiss with a gasp.

"Oh, fuck you feel good."

"Don't stop," she moaned.

He shook his head. "No condom. I need to. You were just too tempting in that second. Fuck, Lily. It's never felt this good before."

"Please," she whimpered.

"Honey, I need a condom."

"I'm on the pill," she blurted.

He froze, buried in her to the hilt. His cock twitched against her walls. Her own body pulsed, ready for more from him. She could feel the ridges of him, the sensation not dulled by a barrier of rubber between them. She'd never had sex without a condom before. She didn't know it could feel that good. Although she was pretty sure that had more to do with the man inside her than the missing condom.

"Lily," he groaned.

"I'm clean, Archer. I haven't been with anyone in a long time and I've been tested. And I trust you."

"Lily, you barely know me."

"I know you're Jaymes's brother. I know you came when I

called. I know you'd do anything for your brother. And I know you'd never lie to me. If you say it's okay, I trust you."

"Lily."

She could see the battle behind his eyes. He didn't want to stop to put on a condom, but he was worried. About himself? She didn't think so. He was worried about her. About keeping her safe.

"Please, Archer. Let me feel you. Just you."

She clenched her channel around him, and he snapped. He claimed her lips, diving into her with everything he had. His hips pistoned against hers, driving deeper and deeper into her until she had no choice but to pull away from his kiss so she could breathe.

"Oh, fuck. Archer. Yes, yes, yes! Oh, shit. Now! I'm coming now!"

She came all at once, with no warning or chance to prepare herself. She screamed and moaned and bit his shoulder.

He hissed a breath, then pumped harder into her, holding nothing back. Just as she was starting to recover from her orgasm, he reared up, lifting her hips with him. He hit her in a whole new place and started the process all over again.

She struggled for breath, trying to drag enough oxygen into her lungs. She panted and moaned and met his thrusts, racing toward the same release he was chasing.

He reached for her breasts and squeezed them tight, using them as leverage to thrust deeper into her. She screamed, then came hard, seconds before he yelled her name and filled her.

He drove into her a few more times, his body twitching with the effort, then collapsed onto her. He rolled them after a few seconds, staying inside her as they moved. She tried to move off him, but he wouldn't let her go.

When he shrank enough to slip out of her, he rolled them again and unlocked the door and went to the bathroom. He came back a minute later with a warm washcloth and cleaned between her legs. She thought to fight him, but she didn't have the strength.

He took the washcloth back to the bathroom, then slipped between the covers with her again. He kissed the side of her head and tucked her against his side. "Get some sleep, sweetheart."

She nodded, already halfway there. For just a minute, she could believe what they had could last.

ARCHER LAID STILL until Lily's breathing lengthened and slowed. Even then, he stayed in her bed, afraid to break the spell the two of them were in.

He'd never had sex without a condom. Ever. He never would have thought to do it either, but she asked, and as soon as she said it, he couldn't think about anything else.

She felt amazing. Every inch of her welcomed him in, enveloping him so completely that he couldn't fathom a life without her. He was in way over his head.

He slid out of her bed and grabbed his shorts and shirt. He stepped into the shorts as he eased the door open, then tugged his shirt over his head. He took one last look at her and pulled the door closed behind himself.

He tiptoed past Jack, even though he knew Jack wasn't asleep, and lifted Lily's keys from the table. With his sneakers on, he headed out the door, needing some fresh air to think things through.

The chilly blast woke him up even more than the sound of Lily screaming his name. Archer tied his sneakers tight and took off at a run toward the entrance to the apartment complex. It had been too long since he'd been out for a good midnight run. In DC, he did his running in the morning. In the desert, he always ran in the middle of the night. It was the only time the horrible desert was reasonably cool enough not to choke you just for thinking about it.

Archer turned to the right and headed away from the heavy traffic areas. There were enough side streets through the neighborhood that he could get in a good four or five mile run without having to go onto a main road.

Before long, the rhythmic pounding of his feet on the pavement cleared his mind. He couldn't think with Lily in there. Running let him concentrate on his brother. All they knew was he was writing a new code for the power plant. From what Archer knew, if the code worked in one plant, it would work in the other as they had similar set-ups. Whoever was behind the whole thing had to be going after the power plants. It was the only thing that made sense.

But even that didn't make sense. There had to be a reason. A why. Something they were missing.

If Dunn would get his head out of his ass and realize Lily wasn't a suspect, he might be able to figure out what was really going on. Instead, Dunn was convinced Lily was going to screw them the same way his CI did in the desert.

Dunn got too close. He started talking about protecting her, bringing her to the States. Hiding her. He stopped seeing her as someone who was helping them for a price and saw her as someone who was helping them because she wanted to.

He was wrong. She could be bought, something they

learned the hard way when she sold them out. Three members of the team paid for it with their lives.

Rodney died the same night.

Dunn didn't trust anyone again. Not really. He was there for Archer, but only because he was in the same fight Archer was. Dunn knew the shit storm that went down that night, what they faced. He understood how easy it was to shoot the wrong target. It didn't matter that the target was wearing the same uniform as the rest of them. Archer fucked up. Dunn fucked up. And the two of them would pay for it the rest of their lives.

Archer kept running, thinking over everything until he knew they had no choice but to dig deeper into the power plants, all their employees, and any contractors hired like Jaymes was. It was a big job, but they had no choice if they were going to find Jaymes before whoever held him spilled the rest of his blood.

17

LILY WOKE UP EARLY THE NEXT MORNING TO A DELICIOUS tingle between her thighs. Archer woke her up a few hours after she went to sleep smelling like he'd just taken a shower. He got dirty all over again with her, then wrapped her in his arms and passed out.

She thought he'd still be there when she woke up, but he was already gone. Muffled voices told her Jack was awake also, just like the morning before.

Lily got dressed and opened her door. It swung open silently, letting her hear what they were saying without them realizing she was there.

"That's a lot of people to look into," Jack said.

"I know. But it's the only lead we have."

"It sucks not having the resources we're used to."

Archer laughed. "Tell me about it."

"Are you going to tell Lily?"

"About the power plant?"

There was a pause. Blood roared in Lily's ears as she waited for his answer. If he was willing to tell her what he knew, he trusted her. If he didn't...

"I know Dunn won't want her to know. Part of me doesn't want to tell her so he can't say she had anything to do with it. But I trust her. I know she's not behind this."

"Because you've had your dick inside her?"

Archer growled. "No. Because I trust her. She's a good person. She loves my brother."

"What's going to happen when he comes back?"

"With what?"

"With the two of you. Are you staying here?"

Lily wished she could see Archer's face when Jack asked him the question.

"I hated growing up here. I couldn't wait to get the hell out of town. I'm only here now because of Jaymes."

"So when we find him, you're gone again."

Archer sighed. "I guess. There's no reason for me to stay here."

"What about Lily?"

One of their phones rang before Archer could answer the question. Lily ducked into the bathroom. She really wanted to know the answer to Jack's last question. Would Archer stay for her?

She used the bathroom, then stared at her reflection as she washed her hands. Her hair was matted on one side and tangled on the other. Her neck had a red patch from his whiskers. She was sure there was a matching redness between her thighs. Her panties dampened at the thought. The sex was amazing, even though they'd only known each other a couple of days. So was everything else with Archer.

She didn't know what to think or how to feel. She could see herself falling for him, even though she never imagined she'd feel that way. For the first time ever, she understood how her mother could get so wrapped up in whatever guy duped her into marrying him.

Lily never wanted to be like her mom, latching on to any guy who paid her attention. Her mom went through three husbands and two live-in boyfriends since Lily's dad left when she was twelve. When she was in between men, Lily was her support system. She hated it. Every time one of them left her, she turned to Lily for support and advice. She was the reason Lily learned to bake. Her mom wanted sweets when she was dumped. Cookies, cake, brownies, ice cream, anything that was more sugar than anything else. It was up to Lily to provide it, so she learned to bake.

When Lily really needed someone, she turned to Archer. Sure, it was a logical choice, but sleeping with him had nothing to do with logic and everything to do with hormones. He made her feel safe and beautiful and wanted. He wasn't particularly charming, but he was protective and possessive where she was concerned. She'd never known a man like him before.

And in just three days, she thought she was in love with him.

She was a fool.

THE BATHROOM DOOR opened as Jack hung up the phone. Archer turned to see Lily, watching as she tied her hair back into a ponytail. With her neck exposed, he could see the marks he left on her skin the night before. The pale contrast with the red burn stirred a possessive and a guilty war within him.

He walked over to her, forgetting about Jack with Lily there, still warm and rumpled from her sleep. He nuzzled against her cheek and whispered, "I'm sorry I hurt you." He trailed his fingers over the mark so she knew what he was talking about.

She wrapped her arms around his waist and burrowed into his chest. "It doesn't hurt. It's a nice reminder of other places where I have that same mark."

Archer's cock twitched. He had a damn good memory of where else she had that mark. He couldn't wait to make it again and again. "You're a tease."

Lily laughed softly, her body shaking gently against his. "Teasing myself, too. I'm still sore all over."

"I'm sorry about that, too."

She shook her head. "No, you're not."

He grinned. "You're right. I'm not."

"Guys?" Jack interrupted. "We need to head out."

"Did you find something? Did you find Jaymes?"

Jack slid Archer a look. He was letting Archer make the call about what to tell Lily. Good man.

"No. Unfortunately, we didn't. Dunn has a few thoughts, and he wants to talk about everything."

"And I'm to stay put, right?"

Archer grimaced and nodded. "Yeah. I'm sorry."

Lily shook her head and stepped back. "It's fine. I understand. I'm going to get ready for work. Then you won't have to worry about me accidentally overhearing anything."

"Are you sure it's safe there?"

Lily huffed. She was annoyed with him, probably for more than a couple of reasons. "I'll be fine. I was fine yesterday."

"I'll drive you," Archer said.

Lily shook her head. "No. Find Jaymes. Go upstairs and find out what they know. Find your brother and bring him home. If you're with me too much, they're going to think I'm guilty. It's best for Jaymes if you stay away."

Archer hated that she was right. He knew the only way for Dunn to trust her was to cut her completely out of the loop. He hated to do it, but it was for the best.

"I'm not staying away, but I will keep my mouth shut. It's only to protect you, Lil."

She nodded but didn't look convinced. "I know. I'll see you this afternoon."

Archer nodded and watched her go. She closed and locked the bathroom door. The shower turned on a second later.

"I fucking hate this," Archer mumbled.

"I know," Jack said. "She's been nothing but awesome. Dunn's being an asshole, but he's the head asshole so we're listening to him."

"Did you talk to Williams? Maybe he can talk some sense into Dunn."

Jack shrugged. "Worth a shot. If anyone can make sense of Dunn, it's definitely Williams. Let's head up and see what's going on."

Archer gave the closed door one last glance, then followed Jack out the door and up the stairs to Jaymes's apartment.

The room was buzzing when they walked in. Dunn paced as he talked on the phone, English tapped away at his keyboard, and Slade and Rocky stood toe-to-toe in the middle of the living room. Just a typical day in the office.

"All right, all right," Jack said, stepping between Slade and Rocky. "What the hell is going on?"

Williams was in the kitchen pouring himself a cup of coffee. He was as hooked on his caffeine as he was on the military. Archer smiled, reminding himself that some things never change.

"Did Dunn tell you what he said to Lily last night?" Archer asked Williams quietly.

They leaned against the counter side-by-side and watched the mayhem in the rest of the place. If Jaymes's apartment survived the eight of them it would be a minor miracle.

Williams nodded. "He did. I'm sorry. Is she okay?"

Archer shrugged. "Feels like shit. She didn't do it."

Williams clapped him on the shoulder. "I know. I think Dunn does, too. He's gun shy."

"I know. And I get it. But why her?"

Williams gave him a grin. "Because she's the perfect target. She has the skills as an IT person, she's the one who brought you into this, and she had the opportunity."

"You sound like you believe him," Archer accused.

Williams shook his head. "No. I don't. I know it wasn't her. But I also know Dunn won't stop until he finds out what's really going on."

"He's looking into the power plant."

"Yep."

"Do you think that's a good call?"

"Absolutely. If your brother was doing something with them not long ago, it makes sense that the plant could be a target for whatever this is. Between the US and Canada, those plants supply power for a huge portion of the area. Taking them out would be devastating."

Archer nodded. "It would be. I'm just trying to figure out why anyone would do this with computers, though. If you want to blow them up, set charges."

Williams shook his head. "The tunnels are too far underground. And the plants themselves are only part of it. You have to take out the whole system. From the tunnels to the dams to the turbines and everything else.

Hydropower is a complicated animal, especially on this magnitude."

"You sure know a lot about this place. When did you become an expert?"

Williams chuckled. "They have a lot of info on their website. All you have to do is read it. Plus, they have a visitors center."

"Really? Do you think any of this would be going down there?"

Williams shook his head. "They wouldn't need your brother if it was. It's more complicated than that."

Archer watched the rest of the room as they searched. He knew English was doing a background check on all the employees and contractors. Dunn was likely calling in whatever favors he could get out of anyone he knew. Slade and Rocky stopped arguing and were laughing at something Jack said.

They all played their roles. Jack was the one who kept everyone laughing. Rocky mothered everyone, as evidence by the biscuits on the table and the sausage gravy in a small crockpot next to them. A good southern boy always fixed hearty food. Dunn took charge and led them. Dex was right behind Dunn, listening to his conversation and adding his own comments for Dunn to relay to whoever was on the phone. English stayed behind his laptop more than his gun, although he was equally deadly with both. Slade was the one they could always count on for a dirty joke and a string of broken hearts behind him. He was the kind of guy everyone wanted to know, men and women. Williams stood back and let them figure things out on their own. He was a leader that allowed you to fall flat on your face a few times but was always there to pick you back up.

"Have you seen the girls since you've been out?" Archer

asked. He knew Williams' divorce was messy, but he loved his daughters. If he had to guess, he went straight to their house when he landed and barely left since.

Williams slid him a look and shook his head.

"Really? Why not? They love their daddy."

"They don't think of me as their daddy anymore. Lauren's new husband has taken my place."

"Fuck that. Go get them back."

Williams nodded. "I'm working on it."

"Yeah? Well, good. He shouldn't get to say what happens with them. You're their father."

"I couldn't agree more. I'm not backing down until they're back in my life. I didn't walk away from my career to watch that son of a bitch raise my kids. They're my kids."

"That's FUBAR. I can't believe Lauren did that to you."

Williams laughed mirthlessly. "Lauren is no different than any other woman. She found a new dick to sit on and went for it. She doesn't care about me. Probably never did. Saw a military guy and thought I'd protect her from her abusive father. Now she's with this new fucker and thinks she can just push me out of her life. She's wrong."

Archer wasn't expecting such hostility from Williams, but it was justified. If he dedicated his life to serving his country and his wife of almost twenty years dumped him via a letter when he was overseas, then cut him off from his kids, he'd be pissed, too. More than pissed. He'd be out for blood.

"What are you gonna do about it?" Archer asked.

Williams grinned. "What we always do. Eliminate the threat."

Archer stepped back. "You're not talking about killing him, are you?"

Williams rolled his eyes and shook his head. "No. Of

course not. I'm just going to make sure Lauren sees him for who he really is. When she knows the truth, she won't want him anywhere near our girls."

Archer grinned. Something about the way Williams said it set him on edge, but he was probably reading too much into it. Williams said he wasn't going to hurt the guy, and if he was hiding something from Lauren, she deserved to know.

He was sure it was nothing. Williams was a good guy. He wouldn't do anything illegal.

"I have a list," English announced to the room.

Dunn told the person he was talking to he had to go and the rest of the team gathered around English's computer for the report.

"I'd start with these three. All of them were involved with Jaymes and the project he was working on. They all have criminal records. And they all have pensions with the company that tanked a few years ago."

"So motive?"

English nodded. "Good ones."

"Who are they?"

"Chris Paulo. Roger Franklin. Bryan Jenson."

English handed driver's license photos to Dunn. He flipped through them. "We need to look into these guys. Go to their houses. Keep an eye on them. Time is of the essence here so let's split up. I'll take Paulo."

"Give me Franklin," Williams said.

"I'll take Jenson," Dex said.

"Good. Team up. Let's find this bastard. Ford, you're with me."

Archer traded a look with Jack as Jack went to look over the intel Williams had. Slade joined Dex and they all dove in.

"Divorced, three kids. Two are adults, one is still in college. Looks like he got into a few bar fights in college," Dunn said, reading the background English handed over on their guy. "Manslaughter charge was dropped when he went to rehab. Looks like it was just after his divorce. Figures."

"What does that mean?"

"Means women fuck everything up."

Archer bristled. "Why are you so set on her being the bad guy here? You don't even know her."

"Yeah? Neither do you. Just because you put your cock in her doesn't tell you anything about the woman."

Archer didn't think, he just swung. Hard. He was known as the muscle in their group, and he used every fucking one he had to beat his XO until someone pulled him off.

Dunn fought back, landed a few good blows, but he definitely got the worst of it. Archer shrugged off Jack and Dex, tossing glares at both of them, and wiped the blood from his lip. His cheek hurt like a son of a bitch, but he knew Dunn's had to be worse.

Good.

"When she ends up on the wrong side of this one, you can apologize."

"When she ends up on the right side, you can kiss my fucking ass," Archer spat back. "I'm not working with you. Slade, trade with me."

Slade shrugged and reached for the papers Dunn dropped on the floor while they fought. Dunn turned his back on them and looked at Dex.

"What's this one?"

"A few B&E's, shoplifting. Lives with his mom in the house he grew up in. Been at the plant for almost thirty years. He didn't take the payout for the pension plan, but with the changes, he's not going to see much. If he'd taken the payout five years ago, things would have been different."

"Money makes people do crazy things," Archer grumbled.

"Yep. Looks like this guy is at work right now, according to his cell, but no one's home. Want to go check out his place?"

Archer nodded. "Hooyah."

18

—————

Dex snuck around to the back door while Archer stood out front looking at his phone. The street was quiet, but they weren't taking any chances.

"I'm in," Dex said through the earpiece.

"Open the front," Archer replied.

A few seconds later, the front door opened and Archer walked in like he was supposed to be there.

"You go up. I'll go down," Dex instructed.

Archer nodded and headed for the stairs off to the right. He took them quietly, just in case someone was there even though their intel said the place was empty.

The first bedroom was definitely Jenson's mom's room. A pink robe hung on the back of the closet, makeup was spread out across the dresser, and a bra was draped over the footboard of the bed. Archer did a quick sweep, then moved to the next room.

A spare bedroom, hall bathroom, and exercise room took up more space until Archer reached the end of the hall. He opened the last door carefully, leading inside with his gun drawn. The room was vacant but had enough computer equipment to give English a boner.

"Holy shit," Dex murmured through the coms. "You gotta see this."

"On my way, then I have one for you."

When Archer found Dex in the basement, he stared at the wall with him.

"What the hell?"

"This guy means business."

Archer snorted. "Something like that. I've never seen that many dolls. What are they wearing?"

Dex shook his head, fighting his own laughter. "Panties. Women's panties as dresses."

"Ex-girlfriends?"

Dex shook his head. "I doubt he has that many. What does he even do with them?"

"I'm not sure I want to know. How long ago do you think he started this collection?"

Dex snickered. "Looks like a while. I wonder if these are the only friends he's ever had."

Archer laughed. "He fits the profile of a whacko, that's for sure."

Dex snorted, then apologized. "Sorry. I know we're looking for your brother."

Archer ran a hand down his neck. He'd had a kink in it since he woke up and had to face Dunn and the others. Stress. The only thing that brought him any kind of relief was Lily, and he had to cut her out of all this shit so they didn't blame her.

"It's just a shitty situation. Even more since Dunn's out to get Lily."

"You know how he is," Dex argued, heading for the stairs

to take them out of the basement. "His head's still all messed up."

"That doesn't give him blanket rights to blame Lily."

Dex shook his head. "No. It doesn't. And we told him that last night."

Archer snapped his head up to look at Dex. "Thanks. That means a lot."

Dex nodded. "You can see the fear in her eyes. She's trying to hold it together, but she's scared. She really loves your brother."

Hearing the words was like a punch to the gut. Archer knew Lily and Jaymes were close, but she convinced him he was just her best friend. If Dex saw more in her, maybe he was wrong. Maybe he was just a substitute for his brother.

"You know that, though. She's got to be scared out of her mind."

Archer nodded and led the way up the stairs to the computer room he found. When they walked inside, Dex finally stopped talking about Lily.

"Well, fuck me sideways."

"Yeah, that's what I thought."

"If he has all this shit, why does he need Jaymes? I'd guess he's pretty computer savvy himself."

Archer nodded. "Exactly. You know if we go back without a copy of his hard drive English'll flip out."

"True. Download it all and let's get out of here."

Archer slid a thumb drive into the USB port on the front of the computer. A few clicks on the mouse and the entire drive was copied, including all the hidden files.

They were back in the hallway and heading toward the stairs when the front door opened. Archer and Dex looked at each other and ducked into the bathroom. They closed themselves behind the shower curtain, listening as the guy on the phone came closer and closer to them.

"I know. Yeah. I get it. Okay. No. Don't do that. I can handle it. I can. Give me a couple days and I'll have the money for you."

Archer and Dex traded silent looks. Dex slid his phone out of his pocket and hit the record button so they could capture Jenson's side of the conversation.

Jenson followed them into the bathroom. He left the door open while he talked, his voice echoing through the small space.

"I came to you first. Why would you do that? You can't cut me out of this. No. Okay, tomorrow. I'll have the money for you tomorrow. Just don't cut me out of it."

The guy took a leak, then left the bathroom without washing his hands. His voice trailed off as he went down the stairs again.

"Let's go," Dex whispered.

They ducked out of the shower curtain and hugged the wall until they hit the first floor. Archer froze when he heard the guy cooing to someone.

"There's someone else down there," he said.

Dex stilled, listening. Another voice, high-pitched and feminine sounding, said something.

"Fuck. He could be holding her prisoner. We need to check it out."

Dex nodded and swore. They eased across the well-worn floors to the basement steps. Archer could see Jenson if he laid down and peeked under the support for the first floor. Dex mimicked his pose.

Jenson lifted one of the dolls and nuzzled it close to his slender face. His greasy hair was slicked back, a week or more growth on his cheeks. He sat on a gray metal chair, the tail of his shirt falling below the edge of the seat. His pants drooped off him. Everything looked like he was a little kid playing in his dad's dresser.

He kissed the doll and cooed again.

Then he said, "I wish you would play with me more. I get so lonely down here."

Archer swung his gaze to Dex and stifled a laugh. Dex's eyes flashed with humor. He pressed his lips together and backed up.

Archer followed his movements until they were on their feet. They snuck out the front door and walked calmly to Archer's truck. Only then did they start laughing.

"He was talking to them. Holy shit. I almost lost it back there," Dex said, doubling over with laughter. He rested his forearm on the dashboard and laughed until tears ran down his face.

Archer was right there with him, struggling to breathe. The image of that guy, hunched over on his chair, talking to himself as the doll wrapped in panties, was just too funny.

"Well, we definitely know he's not our guy," Dex said when he finally stopped laughing. "I doubt he can piece together two sentences on his own besides to his toys."

That set them off again. Archer started the truck and chuckled the entire drive back to Jaymes's apartment.

It wasn't long before everyone was back from their searches with info.

"Jenson was a bust," Dex told the others. "He had a room full of computers that told us he could have done the job without help if he wanted to, but the clincher was when he started talking to his dolls. The guy has no social skills, and that's being generous. He's a bit off, but I don't think he's dangerous."

"Okay, so he's a no go," Dunn said.

Dex and Archer traded a look and shook their heads.

"I think our guy is the same. He was hanging out in a bar so we bought him a couple drinks and talked to him. We didn't get the feeling he was interested in anything other than finding a woman to take home for the night and another beer. Not a real deep thinker," Dunn explained.

"Guess rehab didn't stick. That's two down," Dex said. "What about Franklin?"

All eyes swung to Williams and Jack. Jack stepped forward.

"Looked like a nice guy on the surface. Wife, couple teenagers. We got into his house and had a look around. Found a stash of weapons in his basement hidden under a tarp near the back. Had some high tech coms down there, too. Not the kind of shit an innocent guy is going to have."

Archer's gut rolled.

"Anything that would point us to Jaymes?" Dex asked.

Jack shook his head. "Unfortunately, no. But I think it's reasonable to keep an eye on this guy."

"English, any luck with video on the last site?" Dunn asked.

English shook his head.

"What video?" Williams asked.

Dunn turned to him. "I asked him to look for anything that could help us see where the people who have Jaymes took him before we showed up."

"Yeah," English broke in, "but the area is so deserted that there aren't any cameras I can tap. The few in the area didn't catch anything at that bunker so all I can do is follow every car that left the cemetery within a few hours of us getting there. And even that we don't know who we're watching. It isn't like there weren't funerals."

"Yeah, but if anyone left and went to other deserted

areas, it could tell us something," Archer said, moving to look over English's shoulder.

"Yeah, but none did."

"Where did they go?"

"Mostly residential. Going home after the funeral or work. Some went over the border. A handful went—"

"Wait, the border?" Archer said. "I thought we were thinking this could be something that attacks both sides. Is it possible they moved their operation to Canada?"

The silence in the room was only the calm before the storm. English started tapping keys. Dunn pulled out his phone. Everyone else started talking.

They were finally on to something. Archer could feel it. He was going to bring his brother home. Alive. Something he couldn't do for Rodney.

ARCHER WAS WATCHING the clock as it ticked closer and closer to six. Lily should have been home, but she wouldn't check in with him. She'd keep her distance so Dunn didn't lay into her again.

"Got a sec?" Dunn asked. "Let's go for a walk."

Archer raised an eyebrow at him but nodded. He was still one of the few people Archer trusted with his life. He was pissed at him, but he trusted him. It was a painful battle.

They walked down the stairs and out into the sunshine in silence. Archer didn't know where they were going to walk, but he set off toward the road. If nothing else, they could walk the neighborhood.

Dunn was silent the first few minutes. Archer wanted to push him, but poking a caged animal was never smart.

"I was wrong."

Archer swung his gaze to his XO in shock. "About?"

"Lily. She wasn't to blame for any of this. I know it, but I didn't want to admit you could pick a woman and I couldn't."

Archer snorted. "She sort of fell into my lap. I didn't pick her."

"Yeah, but you trust her. You know she's good. You never doubted her for a second, and you were right. I never doubted Ashaki. I thought she was telling the truth the entire time. It never occurred to me she would double cross us. Double cross me."

"What happened?" Archer asked. He'd never had the guts to question the details before. Didn't care either. He was too lost in his own grief, and guilt, over Rodney. The specifics didn't matter when his best friend and brother was dead. Especially when it happened at his hand.

"I thought we had something. I was stupid. She played me. The whole time she played me. She always said she wanted to talk to me. I thought it meant something. But it was just a lie to get me to tell her things so she could trade those secrets to the other side."

"She knew about the raid?" Archer asked, even though he already knew the answer.

Dunn nodded. "I told her. I didn't think it was a big deal. She was the one who told us where they would be. I figured she knew we'd be there, so when she asked about it, I confirmed without questioning her why she wanted to know."

Archer shook his head. He was solely to blame for Rodney's death. He was the one who pulled the trigger. But Dunn was the reason they were there in the first place, then ambushed. He was the one who got the intel. He was the one who fucked up with the CI. He was the one who made it possible for their Team to be attacked.

"Rodney didn't deserve to die."

Dunn sucked in a breath. "I know. And I'll take that guilt with me the rest of my life. You might have been the one who pulled the trigger, but I put the gun in your hand and told you to shoot. You were following orders."

Archer's chest tightened at Dunn's words. He meant them to be comforting, but they had the opposite effect. Archer hated hearing Dunn say them. It was the first time he'd ever accused Archer of killing Rodney. The first time Archer felt like he was guilty and had gotten off easy.

"I didn't mean to kill him," he muttered.

Dunn stopped and turned to him. "I know."

"You don't sound like you know. You sound like you want someone to blame instead of yourself. Like you're better than me because you weren't the one holding the gun and squeezing the fucking trigger. Fuck you, Pres."

Dunn's dark eyes went murderous. Every muscle in his body tightened. His hands curled into fists.

Bring it on.

"I'm out here trying to apologize for thinking your girlfriend was pulling all the strings here, and you're being a fucking asshole. What the hell is the matter with you?"

"You. You're not invincible, but apparently I'm supposed to think you are. Did you ever give a second thought to your accusation?"

"What accusation?"

"Exactly! You don't even realize what you said. You're too busy trying to be in charge. You're not my XO anymore. You're a civvie, just like the rest of us. You can't control anything."

"If I'm so fucking useless, why am I here?"

Archer shrugged. "Hell if I know. All you've done is chase away the one person who could give us any good information about my brother. English pretty much did the rest of it."

Dunn glared at him for a long moment. Archer thought about apologizing for point three seconds before he dismissed the thought. Dunn needed to hear what he said. He wasn't going to take it back.

"If you knew anything about your brother, you might have been that source of information. But we all know you can't keep anyone safe. Never could, never will."

Archer didn't think, he just swung. His fist connected again with Dunn's jaw, but Dunn was ready for it. He swung back immediately, catching Archer off guard and knocking him to the ground.

Archer scrambled to his feet and squared off with his friend. His XO. Someone he never thought he'd stand on the opposite side from.

"I guess I should just get out of your way then. Head out of town," Dunn said, rubbing his jaw.

Archer crossed his arms over his chest and flexed his muscles. "Probably for the best."

A flash of red came toward them down the street. Archer stepped into the road and flagged her down. Lily slowed and stopped for him. He gave Dunn one last glare and got in the car with Lily.

Fuck Dunn. Archer didn't need him. He'd find his brother and save him without someone else telling him what to do.

19

———————

Lily didn't say anything as Archer folded himself into her tiny Civic. He was obviously pissed off, and if the bruise on his cheek was any indication, the redness beneath his eye wasn't the first punch he'd taken that day.

"Just drive," he said right before she turned into her complex.

Lily flicked the blinker off and kept going. Her stomach growled, but she was more worried about Archer than how hungry she was. She headed toward Goat Island, the one place she always felt made everything better.

They crossed the bridge and entered the park. She found a parking spot near one of the trails and turned off her car.

"I haven't been here in years."

Lily smiled. Sometimes she forgot Jaymes and Archer grew up there since she didn't. She had to learn her way around in college, exploring. A lot of her adventures involved Jaymes. He brought her there one of their first times studying. She thought for a minute he was going to kiss her, but he didn't, and they were best friends every day after that.

"Jaymes and I come here every few weeks just to wander around and talk."

"What do you talk about?"

Lily shrugged. "Whatever's bothering us."

Archer snorted. "I wouldn't know where to start."

They were silent for a few minutes, listening to the roar of the Niagara River on the other side of the trees, rushing past the island that defied gravity and nature.

"My mom called me today. We don't have the best of relationships," Lily said. "That's an understatement. My mom is a challenge on pretty much every level. I love her, but she drives me crazy."

"Where does she live?" Archer asked.

Lily reminded herself she'd only known him a few days. It felt much longer. There was a lot about him she didn't know, and likely never would. She'd shared every inch of her body with him, willingly, but the rest of her was off limits.

Was.

"I grew up in Ohio. Outside Cleveland. Not too far from here, but far enough that my mom won't come for a visit without telling me. Usually because she needs gas money to get here. And food. And a place to stay."

"She's a little demanding, huh?"

Lily laughed mirthlessly. "To say the least. She hasn't been my mom since my dad left. He took care of her so I didn't notice it when I was young, but once he was gone, it was my job to take care of her."

"Take care of her? Is she sick or something?" Archer asked.

Lily shook her head. That would have been easier. It

would have given her something closer to tangible to understand. Not that she wished for her mother to be sick, but she knew it was all in her head, and that she could change if she really wanted to. That was what pissed Lily off the most. Her mother didn't want to change.

"My mom is very demanding. She likes to know someone is paying attention to her. If not, she'll make something up so you will pay attention to her."

"Like what?"

"She was convinced one of her ex-husbands was stealing from her. She had me so paranoid that I called the cops on him and had him arrested and investigated."

"Normal people don't have that kind of power," Archer said suspiciously.

"My best friend from high school's dad is the sheriff."

"Ah, makes more sense now."

"They pulled him over and made something up so they could take him in. They couldn't find anything, but he knew my mother was behind the arrest so he left her as soon as he was out."

"Maybe she was right."

Lily snorted and shook her head. "Not a chance. He was a good guy. One of the best. She thought I was moving on with my life. It was my sophomore year of college and I told her I wasn't coming home for Thanksgiving because Jaymes invited me to spend it with him and his...your mom."

"You went to Thanksgiving?"

Lily nodded. "I go most years. Jaymes went home with me once, and he totally understood why I avoided my mother. She likes to stir up drama."

"So what was today's drama?"

"She thinks her hair stylist is out to steal her latest husband."

"Really?" Archer asked with a laugh.

Lily nodded. "This is my life. It's so fun and exciting. You know you're jealous."

Archer laughed again. "I am. Terribly jealous."

They walked a little while longer in silence. Lily listened to the birds chirping and the other animals rustling the bushes near where they walked. Archer was quiet, but he was thinking really loudly.

"Rodney was my closest friend. We went through BUD/S together."

"Refresh my memory. What is that?"

"SEAL training. Six months of torture, basically. But without it, you're not prepared to be a SEAL."

"Ah, yes. What Jaymes quit. It must be intense."

"It is. Rodney and I were the only two of our original group that made it through. We became like brothers. He had my back, and I had his. We were stationed together and went through everything together. He was going to get married, and I was going to be his best man."

"But?"

"I killed him, Lily. I put a bullet through the back of his head."

Lily gasped. For the first time since she met him, she was a little afraid of Archer. "Why?"

"Friendly fire. That's what they said. We had a CI, a confidential informant. She was working for us and gathering intel on some of the people we were going after. She told us about an exchange that was going to happen. High-profile target. It was a setup and we ended up in a shitty position. When it was all over, Rodney was dead and I was the only one who could have shot him."

Lily breathed again, knowing Archer was being too harsh on himself. "It wasn't your fault."

He snorted. "Dunn just told me it was his fault, except for the fact that he wasn't the one who pulled the trigger. Fucking asshole."

"He's your brother, Archer. He'd do anything for you. Obviously, this isn't something you're going to agree on, but I think you're selling him short. And yourself."

"He all but said I'm the one to blame for Rodney."

"You know that isn't true."

Archer huffed. "It is true. I pulled the fucking trigger. I killed my best friend. I ended the life of the one person I swore to keep safe."

"What are you talking about?"

Archer sighed. He stared off at nothing, his eyes glazing over. "Before we left the last time, Rodney's fiancée talked to me. She asked me to bring him home. To keep an eye on him and watch out for him. She said something was off. That he wasn't acting like himself before we left, and she was worried. She asked me to bring him home, and instead of doing that, I killed him."

Lily knew Archer had killed people. He was a soldier. It was evident in every inch of his well-muscled body. But she also knew he wasn't a murderer. And there was definitely a difference in her eyes. He wouldn't kill someone he considered a friend. He wouldn't kill anyone unless he had to.

The way he beat himself up about it killed her. There had to be more to the story, but she wasn't going to ask.

"You're not a killer, Archer. You're a good man."

"How can you say that?"

"Because the man standing in front of me drove all through the night when I called. You called in people you knew would help when you realized your brother was missing. You've protected me and defended me. You've been everything these past few days. The man I know is not a coldhearted killer who would have done something like this."

Archer shook his head. "There was no one else."

Lily laughed. "There's always someone else. Just because you didn't see them, doesn't mean they weren't there."

AT LILY'S WORDS, fingers crawled up Archer's spine. He'd never even considered that someone else could have pulled the trigger. He was there. He was behind Rodney. He had to be the guilty one.

But what if he wasn't?

Archer's head was spinning. He needed to forget about all of it for a little while. To get away and stop obsessing over his brother and his best friend and the ways he'd failed them both.

Lily's stomach growled loudly, giving Archer the out he needed.

"Let's get something to eat."

She shook her head. "I can make us dinner. Why don't we go home? I mean, to my place."

Archer smiled and tucked a strand of hair behind her ear. "You take care of me. Thank you. You've had a long day, a long few days. Let's go out somewhere. Wherever you want to go."

Lily finally nodded and went back to her car. She drove them to a small diner not far from her place. They ate and talked about nothing and everything. He told her about joining the SEALs and about the guys that were camped out in Jaymes's apartment.

She told him about meeting Jaymes and getting her job

at the hospital. They talked about finding Jaymes and skated around his argument with Dunn.

They were heading back to the apartment when Archer got a call from Jack.

"Where are you?"

"Heading back," Archer said. "Why?"

"We need you here. Now. We think we found him."

Archer glanced at Lily. "You did?"

"Yes. Hurry. It's going to take a while to get to him. I'll explain on the way."

Archer hung up and told Lily, "They think they found him. The guys are getting ready to go now."

Lily gasped. "I'm scared to get my hopes up."

Archer reached across the console and gripped her hand. "I feel the same way."

They rode the rest of the way to Lily's apartment like that, her hand clasped in his. His team was in the parking lot when they parked. Archer missed the feel of Lily's hand when he had to let go and get out.

"We have your stuff," Jack said, nodding toward the SUV.

Archer nodded and turned to Lily. "You okay?"

She smiled. "Of course. Go get your brother."

Archer stiffened when Dunn stepped closer to them. He moved to stand with Lily, putting her slightly behind himself to protect her. He wasn't going to take a chance that Dunn was going to go after her again.

"Lily, I owe you an apology."

Archer reached for her as Lily moved to stand next to him.

"I never should have accused you of being behind all this."

Lily smiled at him. "It's okay. I know you're protecting Archer, and by extension Jaymes."

Dunn shook his head and moved a little closer. Archer started to step between them, but Lily put a hand on his arm to stop him.

Dunn slid Archer a look but stopped. "I was taking out my own shit on you. I wasn't fair. And for that I apologize."

"Thank you, Daniel."

Lily smiled at him, and Dunn finally moved away after a glance at Archer. He turned to Lily and cupped her jaw. "Are you okay?"

She nodded. "I'm good. Go get him."

Archer nodded. "Stay safe."

She laughed. "I think I should be saying that to you."

"Let's go," one of the guys called from the SUV. They were all outfitted with vests and holsters and more in the vehicle.

Archer waved to them and focused on Lily. "I'm coming back, and I'm bringing Jaymes."

She looked up at him with watery eyes. "Good."

He leaned down and kissed her gently, then jumped in the back seat of the SUV and they took off.

Lily watched them drive away and tried to pull in a deep breath. Dunn apologized, which would go a long way toward him and Archer working together to get Jaymes back.

She couldn't help but wonder where they were going. She hated to think of Jaymes somewhere dangerous, but he was kidnapped so there wasn't any way around him being in danger.

Lily made her way to her apartment, startled when Blake opened his door behind her as she slid the key into her lock.

"You scared me," she huffed.

"How are you?" he asked with narrowed eyes.

She smiled. "I'm good."

"Jaymes's brother didn't hurt you, did he?"

She shook her head. "Archer's a good man. He's not going to hurt me."

Blake leaned against his doorframe. "I hope not. I'm surprised I keep missing Jaymes. How is he with you seeing his brother?"

Lily shrugged, trying to pass the whole thing off. She really had no clue what Jaymes would think about her and Archer together. They were only sleeping together, not starting a relationship, so she figured Jaymes wouldn't care, but there was a part of her that thought he might be upset.

"He's okay. He really hasn't said anything about it."

"Hmm. That surprises me. You two are close. I would think he'd have an opinion about who you dated."

"Well, I'm not really dating Archer."

"No?"

Lily shook her head again. "We're getting to know each other. He doesn't live here and he's going home soon."

"He is?" Blake asked, his brow furrowing. "I didn't realize he'd be leaving already."

"He's only in town for a few days. It was kind of an unplanned trip, and he won't have a reason to be here much longer. He'll go home."

Blake checked his phone. "Uh, I gotta go. I'll see you later, Lily." He disappeared into his apartment, closing the door in her face.

Lily shook her head and shrugged. She went to her apartment, surprised by how quiet it was.

Having Archer and Jack living with her for the last few days brought so much livelihood into her life. Sure, they argued and ate everything they found, but she loved having them there.

It was late, and she was anxious. Archer's words kept playing through her head. He was bringing Jaymes home.

She grinned. When he got there, she could have his favorite dessert waiting for him. It would keep her busy while the guys were all gone.

She whistled to herself as she pulled all the ingredients out. Everything went into her mixer, whirred together by the blades. It wasn't long before she was pouring batter into a pan and sliding it into the oven.

Lily sat on the couch and watched while the cake baked. She closed her eyes and grinned. Everything was going to be okay. She was going to get her best friend back. Then she'd find a way to hold on to the man she wanted. She couldn't watch Archer walk away. She wouldn't.

20

———

His phone rang, but he sent it to voicemail. He couldn't take the call with others around.

A ding a few seconds later indicated a text message. He turned it over. Blake. Fuck.

> They found something. She said Ford will be going home soon. What's going on?

> Under control. Get Franklin to work. Now.

> Why?

> Because I fucking said so.

"Everything okay?"

He nodded and tucked the phone away. "Good. Right on schedule."

Archer handed over his passport with the others and answered all the questions the agent asked. They were going into Niagara Falls, Canada to visit the bars. They weren't bringing anything into the country. They were only staying a few hours.

Lies. Every last word of it.

Transporting firearms across the border was a big no-no. They could get in deep shit for it. And if their intel was right, his brother would be in even deeper shit. Because he crossed into Canada illegally. Probably in the trunk of a car. Which meant these guys likely had someone working the borders.

"How are we going to explain how Jaymes got into Canada?" Archer asked Williams.

"We'll figure that out when we get back to the states. Right now, let's just find him."

Archer sucked in a breath and tried to calm his breathing. His pulse was pounding, blood roaring in his ears. He was ready for this, but there was doubt hanging on to all the hope he had. Would he find his brother alive? If they went in there guns blazing, would Jaymes end up getting shot like Rodney did? Could he get Jaymes out safely?

He hated to admit that he had no idea. He wasn't sure of anything.

English gave them instructions from the backseat, guiding them through streets none of them were familiar with. They came to an industrial park and pulled in.

"At the back. Looks like it's the last building."

Williams followed English's instructions until they were in front of a low building that looked like it housed electrical equipment.

"Are you sure?" Archer asked.

English checked again. "This is where the signal came from. The van that left the cemetery came straight here. The cell phone from one of the guys is still inside."

Archer couldn't help thinking they'd gotten a lucky break when Williams spotted a van leaving the cemetery with a fake license plate. Archer never would have spotted the difference in the grainy picture, but it was clear, once English enhanced it, that the I used to be a T. It was a crude change, but enough to throw you off unless you were looking for it.

Thankfully, they were looking for it.

From there, it was easy to track the van across the Lewiston-Porter bridge and into Canada. They drove back to the south and holed up in a tiny building in Niagara Falls, Ontario, near the power plant on that side of the border.

English spotted one guy leaving to get food in the video he was able to tap into, but they were fairly sure more were inside.

Williams turned off the SUV as Dunn parked theirs next to it. The men all piled out, silently dressing for battle.

"We ready for this?" Dunn asked.

Everyone nodded.

"Good. Jack, one of those buildings should be good for overwatch. Rocky, stick with him. English and Slade, take point. Slade will get the door for us. Ford, stay on my six. Dex, you're with Williams."

Everyone agreed to their orders. Jack and Rocky disappeared into the darkness within seconds, searching for a spot to keep an eye on the door. Their unspoken rule was to shoot anyone who walked out that wasn't their team.

Slade and English moved toward the door while the rest of them circled the building to verify there were no other entry points. Slade counted down to detonation, and the pop blew the hinges and gave them easy access to the building that held Jaymes.

Williams went in first with Dex right behind him. They

swung their guns both directions, verifying no one was there, then Archer and Dunn followed them inside.

They worked their way down, floor by floor. It felt eerily silent in the empty space. The further under ground they went, the more the building started to smell.

Mold. Damp dirt. Stagnant water.

There was something else that Archer couldn't figure out. A smell that he knew but couldn't place.

They kept moving. Clearing floor by floor. They'd gone down four when something felt different. Archer could sense a change. Someone was there.

"On alert, boys," Williams said in their ear.

He barely got the words out when the pop of a gun echoed in the small space. Everyone turned toward the source, unloading rounds into the darkness.

Pressed to the walls, all of them eased toward the opening where the gunshots came from. Night vision goggles helped, but there was nothing to see except the flash of gunfire.

Someone yelled, but Archer had no idea which side it came from. They surged forward. There was nothing to hide behind and no way to defend themselves. They had to kill or be killed, and there was no way in hell Archer was going to watch any more of his brothers die.

Williams stepped out from behind the wall and fired off shots. Within seconds, he stopped, lowering his gun.

Silence surrounded them. Too quiet. If his brother was there, wouldn't he be calling for help? Unless he was already dead.

BLAKE HATED BEING KEPT in the dark. He wasn't the one pulling the strings so he had no say in the matter, but he was pissed. He was the one who set everything up, from who they'd take to how they'd get it done. Yeah, he was following orders, but his 'boss' didn't know shit about the area. Or the people. That was all Blake.

He sat in the parking lot and waited for Franklin to show up. How he fit into the whole thing was still a mystery to him, but he knew better than to question it. His brother told him the guy they were dealing with was a cruel son of a bitch. Not that Blake was shocked by that, but shit.

When they first talked, Blake was a hard no. He was not going to destroy the power plants in the US and Canada. He was not going to take out the entire region, and maybe a few casualties along the way. No. But the more the guy talked, the more he made sense.

Blake wasn't military, but he was a government employee. He understood the frustrations with low pay and shitty benefits and what it did to your personal life. Hell, he hadn't had a real relationship in years. Once women found out he worked almost every weekend, they had no interest in trying to make it work with him. He'd given up, choosing to take whatever he could get from a woman. Hell, he didn't need anything more than a place to pump into once in a while.

But none of them stuck. They wanted men with more to offer. House, good job, fancy trips. Shit he'd never be able to afford. Fucking bitches.

Franklin pulled into the lot and parked near the door. Blake didn't like the guy on principle. He had everything. Wife, two kids, good job, nice house. Of course, the kids weren't his, and the wife was new, but he did things the right way. He had the money to buy a house and do all that other shit women liked, so when the woman came along, it was easy for him to slide them right into his life.

Lucky bastard.

Blake's phone buzzed with a new message. He opened it and read through his instructions. Then read them again. None of it made sense.

He called the number back, but he got sent straight to voicemail. That happened a lot. Another thing Blake didn't like about the guy. He sounded older, like he'd be old school. Didn't old school people like to talk more than text?

Blake groaned and sent a text.

Need more info.

Blake didn't have to wait long for a response.

You have a job to do. Fucking do it.

"Fuck you," Blake whispered to his empty car, then got out so he could do his job.

LILY PACED THE APARTMENT, dying for a call from Archer or Jaymes. The cake she baked was cooled and frosted and waiting for Jaymes to come back.

Dread settled in her stomach. She trusted Archer, but he couldn't do anything for his friend, Rodney. There was no way to know if he'd be able to save Jaymes.

Her phone rang and scared the shit out of her. She fumbled with it, dropping it on the carpet. She scrambled to pick it up. "Hello?"

"He's alive."

She sank to the floor and started crying. "Is he okay?"

"Yeah, he's okay. We're on our way home."

"Oh, my God. Thank you, Archer."

Archer breathed heavily into the phone. "You're welcome."

"How far away are you? I want to be there when he gets home."

"We just crossed the border. We'll be there in fifteen minutes."

"The border? He was in Canada?"

Archer exhaled loudly. She could hear the frustration in him, feel his tension through the phone. "Yeah."

"Why?" Lily breathed, more confused by the minute.

"No clue. The guys that had him were shooting at us, and Williams killed them so we could get to Jaymes. We didn't get any information out of them."

"There could be someone else out there."

"We're thinking there is. Someone who was pulling the strings. These guys weren't high level. They were the muscle. The ones that are used and discarded. Replaceable."

"Does Jaymes know who else was there?"

"No. He said he talked to two different guys. One was one of the dead kidnappers, but he said the other guy looked too small to be the one who came in with a mask on."

A chill raced down Lily's back, making her shiver. "I can't imagine what he went through."

Archer sighed heavily. "Yeah, it's not much fun being held captive."

She could tell he was speaking from experience and not hypothetically. Both brothers, held against their will. Both lucky someone was able to save them.

"Tell Jaymes I baked a double chocolate cake for him."

Archer laughed softly and relayed the message. "He's thrilled. I gotta go, babe. I'll see you soon."

Lily hung up and pushed herself off the floor. She couldn't stop smiling. Jaymes was okay. He was safe. No one would take him again.

Lily packed the cake and carried it and her purse upstairs to Jaymes's apartment. She vibrated with nervous energy as she waited for them to get there. When she heard voices and footsteps on the stairs, she had to hold herself back from flinging the door open and rushing out to see him.

The door opened, and Jack walked through first. She peeked around him and saw Archer, then Dex, and finally Jaymes. His chocolate brown eyes found hers and held. He tried to smile, but it turned into wince from the pain. Stubble covered his skin, reminding her how long he'd been gone. A dark slash over his eye matched one on his chin. Between the two, he had a bruise on his cheek that made her gasp. Lily launched herself at her best friend the moment he was inside, wrapping her arms and legs around him.

He groaned at the contact, and she disentangled herself gently. Jaymes didn't let her go.

"We think he has a broken rib. And maybe a concussion. He was lucky," Adrian supplied.

Lily shook her head and cried quietly. Her best friend, the man she counted on, was broken and bruised, and she waited days before calling anyone. If she'd called Archer earlier, Jaymes wouldn't look like he did. He wouldn't be in so much pain.

"I'm so sorry, Jaymes. I'm so sorry. I should have called Archer sooner. I should have gotten you help. I knew something was wrong, but I thought I was being paranoid. I'm so sorry this happened to you."

Jaymes nuzzled into her hair like he'd done hundreds of times before and shook his head. "Nothing to apologize for, honey. I'm safe now. Because of you."

Lily's tears flowed freely, coating her cheeks and chin and soaking Jaymes's shirt. Jaymes kissed her temple and smiled. She was so happy to have him back.

"Are you okay?"

He nodded. "I'm better now that you're here. Did I hear something about double chocolate cake?"

Lily laughed. "You'd never miss a double chocolate cake, would you?"

His eyes sparkled, but there was a darkness in them that was new. It would take a while for Jaymes to be himself again, and Lily was determined to be there for him every step of the way. "Hell no. Good thing they found me when they did. I'd have broken out of there if I knew double chocolate was an option."

Lily laughed. "I wish you had. I was so worried about you."

"Did you get my message?"

Lily snorted. "I did. I knew it was from you."

"Of course. I knew you'd figure it out. Thank you."

"You're not mad I called Archer?"

Jaymes finally looked at his brother. Archer was standing in the kitchen, watching them. Lily smiled at him, but he didn't return the gesture.

"He saved my life. I'm sure you had more important things to do, but thank you for coming," Jaymes said.

Archer nodded once. "I'll let you two be together. You might want to take a shower, but we'll need to talk to you tonight."

"Thanks. I owe you one."

Archer nodded, and Jaymes turned back to Lily. "God, I missed you. I love you so much, Lil."

"I love you, too," she said automatically.

Jaymes pulled her in for another hug and held her close. She burrowed in with her best friend and finally felt like everything was going to be okay. For real this time.

21

Archer left Jaymes's apartment and wanted to punch something. All the times he asked Lily if anything was going on with Jaymes, she said no. That clearly wasn't the case.

Archer stalked down the stairs and outside for something to do. He stopped the bad guys. He did what she asked him to do. Now, he floundered.

Having a mission again, something to do, a place to direct his skills, made him feel like he could handle not being a SEAL. But his job was done. He wasn't needed anymore. He accomplished his task. He could go back to where he came from and let Lily and Jaymes go on with their lives.

He felt like such a fool for thinking she was starting to care about him. The moment she saw Jaymes, she forgot all about him. He was a good substitute, but Jaymes was the Ford she wanted. The one she loved.

Yeah, that fucking gutted him. He finally found a woman he could love, and she wanted his brother instead of him. She said she loved Jaymes, but all she ever asked Archer for was a few orgasms. Served him right, but fuck.

He walked around outside for a while, trying to understand where he went wrong with Lily. She insisted there wasn't anything going on with Jaymes, but you didn't say you loved someone when you didn't. He just got back from being kidnapped. Emotions were high, for everyone. It shouldn't surprise Archer that it took that for Lily to realize she was in love with Jaymes.

The kicker was, Archer didn't blame her. Any woman with half a brain would choose the younger Ford. Smart. Stable. Emotionally sound. Less bullshit and scars and anger. Jaymes was everything Archer would never be. He was exactly the kind of man Lily should be with.

On his way back upstairs, Archer ran into Williams running down. "Whoa, what's wrong?"

Williams cursed and closed his eyes. "Nothing. It's fine."

"Anything we can do?"

Williams laughed mirthlessly and shook his head. "You've all done enough for me. I can handle it from here. Sorry I have to miss the rest of the party."

Archer chuckled. "You sure I can't go with you?"

Williams studied him for a long minute, then shook his head again. "I'm sure. Goodbye Archer."

"See ya."

Archer continued up the stairs and into Jaymes's apartment. The mood was lighter than it'd been since he arrived. Everyone had a beer in their hands, Lily was in the kitchen, and Jaymes was smiling.

It fucking hurt, but Archer knew it was the best-case scenario. His brother was home, and he was going to get the girl.

Jaymes whispered something only Lily could hear, and she smiled up at him and nodded. He hugged her again and kissed the edge of her lips, then headed toward the back of the apartment. A minute later, the shower turned on.

"You want a beer?" Jack asked, handing one to Archer.

Archer took it silently, twisted off the top, and took a long swig.

"Feel better?"

Archer snorted. "Not even close."

"You know how this sort of thing goes. Sucks you got caught up in the middle."

Archer shrugged. "She's where she belongs."

Jack examined Archer for a long moment. "I think she's high on emotion right now."

"What the hell happened to you? Weren't you the one telling me women aren't worth it?"

Jack shrugged. "Maybe some of them are."

Archer stared after Jack as he walked away and joined the rest of the conversation. Archer sat on the outside of the crowd, feeling more and more pissy as the mood grew lighter and lighter. It wasn't a fucking win. There was still someone out there.

"Hey, will you help me?" Lily asked with a touch on his arm.

He shrugged her off and followed her and her hurt expression back to the kitchen.

"Are you okay?"

He forced a smile that didn't fool either of them. "I'm great. What do you need?"

"Well, I was going to kiss you and thank you for bringing Jaymes back."

Archer snorted. "You're welcome."

"What's wrong with you?"

"With me? Nothing. I'm good."

"You're acting like you're mad at me. What did I do?"

Archer shook his head and sneered at her. "Do you really think you can play me like that? That I didn't notice you hanging all over my brother? Kissing him and hugging him and saying you love him?"

"What are you talking about?"

"I'm talking about you and Jaymes. You're not going to balance both of us. I don't share, and I sure as fuck don't share with my brother."

Lily's back stiffened. Her gaze hardened into a harsh glare. "That's true. You don't share. You couldn't share any glory with him as a kid and broke his arm, and now you're acting like a brat all over again. You want everyone to hang all over you and say you're the hero when he was the one who was missing? I missed him. He's my best friend. And instead of me being allowed to be happy he's home, I have to dance around your fragile ego? Screw you, Archer."

Archer drained the rest of his beer and grabbed another one. "Been there, done that. I'll hand you back over to my brother now that he's home. He's the one you wanted all along. I was just a good substitute."

"Not that good," she spat.

Archer nodded once and turned away, going back to the living room to lose himself in the conversation that flowed around him.

Lily was no different than any other woman he knew. Which only reminded him that he never should have gotten involved with her in the first place.

Lily wiped her tears on her sleeve and stirred the sauce in the pan. Spaghetti was a good meal she could make for everyone without taking much time or being ridiculously expensive.

The ground beef was already in the sauce, with spices and a few vegetables she added for a little more flavor and a touch of healthiness.

She stirred and tried to convince herself Archer was being cruel for a good reason, but she couldn't figure out what that reason could be.

He'd never seen her with Jaymes before. They were close, freakishly close it seemed. Lots of people thought they were together, but the kiss Jaymes gave her before he took his shower was the closest he'd ever come to kissing her on the lips.

All she felt was affection for a friend. Not love like Archer claimed.

Screw him. She didn't need him. He was a jealous asshole who accused her of trying to sleep with both of them. It didn't matter how in love with him she was, if that was what he thought of her, she didn't want to be with him.

The pasta cooked as the guys in the living room talked. The shower turned off as she drained the water and tossed the pasta into the sauce. She was just about to call everyone to eat when Jaymes walked back into the kitchen.

He pulled her in for another hug, wrapping himself around her. He needed to feel safe, to know she was there. He told her he was terrified, but she knew it went deeper than that. He thought he was going to die.

They stood there for a few minutes, wrapped up in each other and oblivious to the rest of the world. He smelled like himself again, spicy with a minty scent instead of sweaty and dirty like when he first got there.

A groan from behind her had Lily peeking over her shoulder. Archer was staring at them, his eyes blazing with anger. He had no right to tell her how to live her life or how to treat her best friend. He could believe what he wanted to about her and Jaymes. They knew the truth, and if Archer couldn't handle her having a close friendship with another man, then he didn't deserve to be in her life.

Hell, he didn't deserve it anyway.

"Like nothing ever changed," Archer growled.

Jaymes nodded. "Got my girl back in my arms. I'm good. So much better than that smelly basement with a gun shoved in my face whenever I didn't do what they told me to do."

"Did you finish the algorithm?"

Jaymes sighed. "I did. I stalled as long as I could, but I thought they were going to kill me. I'm sorry."

"It's okay," Lily assured him. "You didn't do anything wrong."

"Well, not exactly," Archer said. "You could have killed a lot of people. Any idea what the algorithm is for?"

"It allows them complete control over the power plants. Intake, pumps, reservoirs, everything."

"What are they doing with it?"

Jaymes shrugged. "I don't know. The guy who wore the mask only told me to get it done. He didn't share his master plan with me."

"Did they get it into the system?"

"I don't know. I finished it before you got there, but I don't know if they had a chance to get it out of there before you guys came in."

Archer snorted. "So it's all our fault? You might have killed thousands of people, and it's our fault because we weren't there soon enough?"

"I didn't say that," Jaymes argued.

Lily stepped between the brothers, a hand on each of

their chests. She wanted to bury herself in Archer and let him soothe the pain he caused, but holding him back from his brother was the closest she'd come to touching him ever again.

"Back off, Archer. He didn't blame you, or anyone."

"Of course you're defending him. I don't know why that would surprise me."

"Archer!" Jaymes shouted.

Archer shook his head and walked away.

"What was that all about?"

Lily forced the pain down and smiled for Jaymes. "Nothing. Nothing at all."

Jaymes didn't believe her, but he didn't push. They ate dinner and polished off the double chocolate cake Lily made, then everyone started to fade. The adrenaline from going after Jaymes and a shootout with his captors had the guys ready to crash long before Lily felt like she could go back to her bed without crying.

"Will you stay with me?" Jaymes asked, keeping his voice low enough that the rest of the guys didn't hear him.

Lily nodded automatically. They'd spent the night together more times than she could count, and if she'd been the one kidnapped, she'd want someone in the room with her all night.

"Who's where tonight?" Dunn asked. He'd taken Jaymes's room while he was gone and was without a bed now that Jaymes returned.

"I'm going to be up most of the night so you can have the couch," English said.

"I probably will be, too," Archer said.

"I'm not giving up my couch," Jack teased, making a run for the door.

"Lily's going to stay with me so someone can sleep in her

bed tonight," Jaymes said, slipping his arm around her waist.

The room went silent before all eyes slid to Archer.

"Well, fucking fabulous. Then we're all set," Archer said, then slammed his way out of the room.

Jaymes looked at the others and asked, "What did I miss?"

Lily glared at the rest of them. They disappeared quietly, English collecting the computers and following Archer and Jack out the door. Dex unrolled his sleeping bag, and Dunn settled on the couch.

"Nothing," Lily said. "Let's get some sleep."

ARCHER COULDN'T SLEEP. At all. He'd never had that problem before. Not like this. He had nightmares after Rodney died, but this was completely different. He couldn't get to sleep at all. Not in Lily's bed, surrounded by her scent. All he could think about was the way she felt beneath him, on top of him, wrapped around him. She was everything he never thought he'd find.

And she was in bed with his brother.

Jack was asleep on the couch, but if anyone would still be up, it was English. He was in the kitchen with his computer and Jaymes's. He was going through the code Jaymes wrote and trying to hack into the power plant to make sure it wasn't already in there.

"I can't get in."

"You?"

English snorted. "Guess they hired someone smarter than me to set up their system."

"So how do we check their system?"

English shrugged. "We could go ask them."

"Walk up to the door, knock, and ask if the code we have that would destroy their plant is on their system yet? I'm thinking that might get us flagged."

"What choice do we have?"

Archer sighed. "None, I guess. It just feels really dumb."

"Like sleeping with your brother's girlfriend?" English asked without taking his eyes off the computer.

"She said she wasn't with him."

"And now?"

Archer laughed mirthlessly. "She said she's in love with him."

"Ouch."

Archer sank back into the chair and rubbed his eyes. "Yeah."

"Sorry. I know you liked her."

"Yeah, well, I'm not meant for a relationship so it's for the best."

English didn't respond, just clicked the keys.

LILY WOKE up to the buzz of her phone. She kept it on a loud tone so it would wake her up if work had an emergency. She scooted out of Jaymes's hold and grabbed her phone from the nightstand.

Archer.

Can we talk?

I'm not sure I want to talk to you right now.

I'm sorry. I was an ass. I'm jealous. Will you meet me outside?

Lily sighed. She didn't want to talk to him after the things he said to her earlier, but she couldn't deny she was curious what he would say.

Lily slipped out of bed and left her phone on the nightstand to charge. She grabbed her keys and tiptoed past Jaymes and the guys sleeping in the living room. She eased out of the apartment as quietly as possible. The building was quiet as she made her way down the two flights of stairs.

Outside was cool, the nighttime air chilled her skin almost instantly. She wished she'd grabbed a sweatshirt, but they wouldn't be out there long. Knowing her, she'd be in Archer's arms within five minutes.

A noise behind her had her turning back to the door. Instead of Archer, it was Blake.

"Hey. What are you doing out here?"

"The same thing you are," he said, moving toward her.

"What?" She backed up.

"I'm sorry, Lily."

She ran into someone behind her and screamed.

22

———————

ARCHER HAD NO INTEREST IN GOING UP TO JAYMES'S apartment and seeing him and Lily together. He barely got any sleep, and he was in a shitty mood. Seeing the woman he wanted in the arms of his brother was not going to improve it.

"We need to get up there," English said in a tone that had fingers crawling up Archer's spine.

"Why?"

English shook his head. "I hope it's nothing, but we need to go."

Archer traded a look with Jack and both followed English out the door and up the stairs.

The first thing Archer noticed when he walked into Jaymes's apartment was it didn't smell like Lily. There was no bacon frying on the stove, no pancakes filling the air, no coffee brewing. The room was close to silent, and it was never silent when Lily was around.

He thought for a second she might still be in bed with Jaymes, but Archer spotted his brother in the corner of the kitchen pulling toast out of the toaster.

"Where's Lily?" Jack asked.

Jaymes shrugged. "She wasn't in bed when I got up. I figured she was with you guys."

"Fuck," English breathed. "We have a problem."

"What is it?" Dunn asked, moving to see English's computer.

"The guy Williams looked into? It's his ex-wife's new husband."

"What?"

"Roger Franklin. Wife, Lauren Franklin. Daughters, Ann and Linda Williams," English relayed.

"Fuck," Dunn swore, staring at the evidence on the screen. "How did we miss this?"

"He wanted us to. He looked into them. Jack, did you notice anything?"

Jack sighed heavily. "He was acting odd, but you guys know how he is. I didn't think anything of it. He was suspicious of the guy the whole time, but so was I. Shit."

"What does this have to do with Lily?" Archer demanded.

English turned and met his gaze. "I think he took her."

"Fuck!" Archer roared. "How the fuck did this happen?" He whirled on his brother. "You! You were supposed to protect her. She went to bed with you, and you let her leave the room and get taken. What the fuck is wrong with you?"

"You better back the fuck off. I'm not a little kid anymore. You can't pretend I'm the enemy and crawl into your fucking hole. She's my best friend. I love her. So don't you dare get all high and fucking mighty on me that this is all my fault."

"Well, whose fault is it?"

"It's yours," Dex said, holding out Lily's phone. "She has texts from you asking to meet her outside last night."

Archer snatched the phone from Dex and scrolled through the messages. "I didn't send these. This wasn't me. Someone cloned my phone."

Dex shrugged. "That's why she left. What were you two fighting about?"

Archer shook his head. "It doesn't matter. We have to find her."

"Give me the phone," English said. He plugged it into his computer and did something to find where the message came from. It didn't take long for him to say, "There. The phone's still local. Shit. That's the address for Franklin."

"If that son of a bitch took her," Archer growled.

"We don't know if Franklin is the mastermind. It could be Williams."

Archer shook his head. "No. He can't be. He's our CO for fuck's sake. Why would he do this?"

Archer looked at the others in the room. They all shook their heads. They felt the same pain he did. They were all betrayed, but it was personal for Archer. Williams took his brother, then the woman he loved. He could handle losing her to his brother, he couldn't handle losing her at the hand of someone he trusted. Not when he knew what Williams was capable of.

"Let's go. Now."

Dunn shook his head. "We need to figure this out. He's going to know we're coming."

A knock on the door had them all turning to see Rocky and Slade walk in.

"Whoa. What did we just step into?" Slade asked.

"Williams. Have you seen him today?"

They shook their heads.

"He usually meets us for breakfast, but he didn't show today. He didn't answer his phone or the door when we knocked. We had to take a cab over here because the truck's gone," Rocky said. "We thought we'd find him here already."

The others exchanged knowing glances. Archer would rather face Hell Week again before accepting that his CO was behind all this.

"Williams played us. He's the one behind all this. He's been pulling the strings. He was the one who warned the guys holding Jaymes to get him out of there. He killed them so they wouldn't talk. He set this whole thing up."

"That's not fucking funny," Slade growled.

Dunn shook his head. "It's not a joke. The guy we've been looking into, Franklin, he's married to Williams' ex-wife. We think he's been behind this whole thing and is setting this guy up for the fall. He has Lily."

"Wait, what?" Rocky said.

"He took Lily sometime last night. She's gone."

"Fuck," Rocky breathed.

"What are we standing around here for?" Slade asked. "Let's go get him."

"Wait," Dunn said, stopping the group. "Are we sure about this? It's Williams. We've grown up with him. He taught us and trained us. He's been there for us, especially you," Dunn said to Archer. "Are you sure you want to go in there? Are you ready to shoot to kill?"

Lily was so exhausted she could barely keep her head up. They had her legs chained to a chair in a basement. Where? She had no clue. It was nice as far as basements went, but she didn't want to be chained anywhere.

She scanned the code for what felt like the tenth time. It was a long algorithm, and her eyes were starting to cross.

She found the errors Jaymes made early on, little things that most people wouldn't notice, but that would make a big difference when the code was uploaded to the server.

Unfortunately for her, Brady knew about the errors.

Son of a bitch.

She never saw it coming. She really thought he was a good guy. He played her well, and the others. That was what scared her most about the situation she was in. They'd never believe her that it was Brady Williams, their commanding officer, who flipped his shit and was her captor. He was the man behind the mask. And the fucker needed her to fix Jaymes's code.

"Are you done yet?" his booming voice preceded him down the stairs of the basement.

Lily's first instinct when they grabbed her the night before was to fight back, but Brady and Blake were stronger than she was. They easily shoved her in Blake's trunk. She kicked the whole way, but it didn't matter. The next time she saw their faces, they were inside a garage. When she jumped up and tried to fight her way out, Brady punched her. Her cheek still stung.

Lily didn't answer the asshole as he moved closer to her. Unfortunately for her, he was smart. Which meant the fucker brought her coffee and breakfast. And she wasn't the kind of woman who could skip a meal, even if her stomach was tied in so many knots she could barely breathe.

"You need your energy, Lily," he said calmly, like he actually gave a shit about her. "And your boyfriends need you to succeed or they die."

His threat. The only reason she was even trying to fix the code Jaymes wrote. If it was just her, she'd let him kill her, but Brady was smart. He threatened to kill Jaymes and Archer, not caring which one she truly loved.

She couldn't let either of them die. It would be bad enough when Archer found out someone he trusted was behind his brother's abduction. He didn't need to die before he could get even with the bastard for it.

"This has to be done today," Brady reminded her.

"Why? Why is today such a big deal?"

Brady grinned. "Because the man who will go down for this won't be here tomorrow."

"Jaymes?"

Brady laughed and shook his head. "No. Not Jaymes. Unfortunately for me, I underestimated my Team. It won't happen again. I have assurances that they won't interfere this time. I will have my virus long before they figure out where you are."

"They'll find me."

Brady smiled sadly at her. "Yes, dear, they will. But I'm sorry to tell you I won't leave witnesses behind this time. You'll go with the house."

"The house?"

Brady turned and walked back up the stairs. Just before the door slammed shut, he said, "Eat your breakfast. When I come back, I expect you to be done."

Lily screamed, but it didn't do any good. He wasn't going to tell her what was going on. He had no reason to share his plans with her. She was a pawn. A dead one if he had a say.

She had to figure out how to get out of there. If he was going to destroy the house, and intended to leave her in it, she needed an escape.

She really should have paid more attention when Jaymes tried to teach her how to defend herself. She'd die regretting it.

Lily sucked down the coffee and devoured the pastry, then dove back into the code. Her only hope was to finish it, then pray they would leave her alone long enough to get away before they found out she screwed up the code, too.

But what would that mean for Archer and Jaymes?

TWO HOURS LATER, the door opened again. Brady's heavy footsteps hit hard on each step, the sound reverberating up Lily's spine. It was her march. Her march to the firing squad. He was back to collect his files. Files that she had to produce, or he'd kill her best friend and the man she loved. Files that meant she was dead.

Lily refused to look at him as he approached and even squeezed her eyes shut when she knew he was there.

"Lily, look at me."

Her eyes flicked open. Blake, not Brady. She hadn't seen him since he helped Brady get her down the stairs to the basement. Not that she was any happier to see the guy she thought was a friend.

Shit, she *kissed* him.

"What are you doing here?"

"I came to get the file. Did you finish it?"

Lily rolled her eyes and turned away from him. She nodded toward the computer, refusing to meet his eyes. She hated that she did what they said. She saved Jaymes and Archer, but how many other people would die because of what she did?

"Is it done, Lily?" Blake demanded.

"Yes," she yelled. "It's done. I finished the damn thing, and it's correct. You two can use it to destroy the power plants now. Are you happy?"

Blake copied the file from the computer onto a flash

drive and turned to face her. He shook his head. "I never wanted any of this to happen, Lily."

"What did you think was going to happen? Did you think getting hooked up with a psycho like Brady was a good idea?"

"I didn't know who he was. Not at first. All our communication was through email. He was looking for some help and I put him in touch with my cousin."

"Why is he doing all this? Where are we?"

Blake glanced toward the stairs. "He wants revenge. His wife left him because he was never around, and she married a guy who works at the power plant."

"Oh, God. That's who's going to be blamed for this, isn't it?"

Blake nodded. "Yep. He's there with him now. At the power plant. Waiting for me to email this to him."

"Blake, you have to help me. Get me out of here."

Blake shook his head. He pursed his lips together and stared at her. "I can't, Lily."

"Why not? He's gone. You just said so. Why can't you let me go? Tell him I escaped."

Blake glanced around the room. Her gaze followed his, hoping they could come up with something. They had to. She knew Blake. She was in his apartment just a couple days ago. He kissed her. He liked her, she knew he did. He wouldn't let her die.

"Then we can be together," she hedged. "You and me."

His gaze cut back to hers. "Do you think I'm playing here? He killed my cousin. Shot him during Jaymes's 'rescue.' He doesn't care who he hurts. He's going to kill that Franklin guy. After they upload this file, he's bringing the guy back here. He already has charges set all over the house."

Lily stilled. Fear clawed at her throat, demanding she scream. If they were in a house, there could be other houses close. Someone would hear her. They had to.

"Help! Help me! Please, help!"

"What are you doing?" Blake demanded, clamping a hand over her mouth.

Lily bit him hard, and he jumped back, swinging his sore hand around. She screamed again. "Help me! Call the police! Help!"

Blake backhanded her across the same cheek Brady hit. The impact sent shock waves of pain across her entire face. Tears instantly filled her eyes. The metallic taste of blood flooded her mouth.

She glared at Blake but didn't give him the satisfaction of a response.

His eyes were sad, but he didn't say anything before he walked away, leaving her chained to a chair in a basement that would be nothing more than rubble as soon as Brady decided to blow it up.

She was going to die.

23

ARCHER WAS GOING TO FUCKING KILL SOMEONE. HE DIDN'T care who, he just needed to put his hands around someone's neck and watch the life leave their eyes.

Williams was his first pick, but Dunn was becoming a close second.

"You need to do exactly what I say," Dunn growled at him.

They stood toe-to-toe outside the one remaining SUV left in the parking lot at Jaymes and Lily's apartment complex. Archer was fucking done. He had to get Lily back. It was his damn fault she was gone. He was an ass. If he hadn't been a dick to her, there would have been no reason for Lily to leave the apartment when she thought he was apologizing.

He needed to apologize. Then he needed to get the fuck away from her so she was safe.

"I'm going to kill that fucker if I see him," Archer ground out.

Dunn shook his head. "No. You will not. We need him

alive so we can find out exactly what he's planning and protect the city."

"He kidnapped my brother and Lily. He's going to pay."

Dunn nodded. "He is. But he's going to pay in jail."

Archer growled and paced away from Dunn. He wanted to believe that was the right answer, but for a man with means and opportunity, a prison was too good. Williams should be in the ground.

"Can I count on you to listen or are you staying here?"

"Fine."

Dunn glared at Archer for a few more seconds, then nodded toward the SUV. They piled in with the others, all geared up and ready to kick some ass. Archer vibrated with pent up energy. They had no idea what they were walking into. They were fairly sure Lily was at Franklin's house, but Franklin's car was at the power plant.

Dunn insisted on going to the power plant first.

The good of the people, he said. The needs of the many outweighed the needs of the few.

Archer threatened to take his own truck and find Lily. He was outvoted.

Which meant he was crammed into the SUV with Dunn, Jack, Dex, and Slade heading toward the power plant to find Williams and Franklin.

Everyone was silent on the drive. Archer's leg bounced as they avoided city streets by taking the interstate around the city north toward the power plant. They followed the same road that led them to the cemetery days ago, turning off at the power plant instead.

Dunn called the plant manager and explained the situation they were facing. The guy thought he was nuts, but Dunn was convincing enough that they were allowed access to the facility. Locked and loaded, the five of them strolled up to the gate with more weapons tucked in their gear than any normal person would realize existed.

Williams would know.

Their only advantage was the element of surprise. If they could get there without Williams realizing they were on site, they had a chance at stopping him.

A small chance, but a chance.

Dunn shook hands with the man in the suit who walked out of the guard shack at their approach. Archer and the others hung back, listening to what they could hear of the uncomfortable conversation between Dunn and the plant manager, Richard Jenkins.

"Franklin isn't answering the phone in his office. We have cameras throughout the facility, but the quality isn't that great so we haven't been able to locate him."

"Do you have cameras in areas where people normally aren't? Tunnels, by the turbines, anything like that?"

Jenkins shook his head. "No. We don't. We've never had this kind of threat before. This facility was built decades ago, and very little has been done to update it. There hasn't been a need."

"I think there's a need now."

Jenkins ran a hand through his short hair and nodded. "Yeah, it appears there is. You have the support of my entire staff. I've notified the executive team of what's going on, but employees are going to lose it when they see the five of you."

Dunn nodded. "We understand. But we need to find them before they destroy this place. They're going to have a computer. Do you have a network that records login locations?"

Jenkins nodded. "We do."

"Get it. It'll give us a place to start looking. Do you have someone who's willing to show us around?"

"I'm going to show you around."

Dunn scanned the man's clothes and shook his head. "Sorry, sir, but are you sure about that?"

Jenkins nodded. "I'm not putting anyone else in danger. This is my facility. I'll get you the information you need and be back here in two minutes."

He ducked into a door behind the security desk with the phone to his ear. The door locked, and they waited.

"Do we trust this guy?" Dex asked as soon as Jenkins was gone.

Dunn nodded. "I think we have to."

"We trusted Williams," Archer growled.

They all sobered at the thought, faces shifting to varying degrees of anger and hurt. Being betrayed stung deeper than anything else. Knowing Williams intentionally put them at risk and took advantage of them... Archer wanted revenge.

The door Jenkins went through opened again, and he walked out in dark blue coveralls, steel toe boots, and a hat tugged low over his eyes.

"Hopefully no one recognizes me and alerts the plant that I'm out there," he said ruefully.

Dunn nodded and accepted the slip of paper handed over.

"His last login was in one of the basements. It's unusual for anyone to be down there, even Franklin."

"Then we'll start there. Lead the way."

They followed Jenkins into the plant and down until they were on a deserted lower level.

"Is there another way off this floor?" Dex asked Jenkins when they all moved forward.

Jenkins nodded. "At the other end of the hall there's a

second elevator and a staircase to the right halfway up. That's all I know about."

"Three exits. Jack?"

"I'm staying here. Can watch the hall."

Dunn nodded, moving forward silently along the damp hallway. Archer's pulse raced, blood roaring in his ears in the silent space.

The murmur of a voice rose above the hum of machines around them.

"There's an office to the left at the end," Jenkins whispered. "That's where the login came from. It's a big room. An old lab. Still connected to the network."

"We need you to stay here," Dunn said to Jenkins. "Jack is watching behind you, and Archer is going to stay with you. Keep you safe."

Archer glared at Dunn. "Why me?"

"You know why."

Archer wanted to argue. It killed him not to. But he was a soldier, and he knew when to keep his trap shut and when to push back.

Most of the time.

Archer moved ahead of Jenkins and pointed his gun toward the door as the rest of the team approached.

"Two people in the room," Dunn whispered through their comms. "Williams has his back to us. The other guy is at a computer. I can't hear them."

"What are we waiting for?" Dex asked.

"Nothing. Going in."

Archer stood outside, his gun trained on the same spot. If Williams walked out that door, he was going down.

Gun fire exploded inside the room, shouting followed. Then silence.

"Do you really want to kill a civilian, Pres?" Williams taunted Dunn. "I didn't think that was your style."

"Why are you doing this?" Dunn demanded.

"You'd never understand. None of you would. You've never lost anyone, had your whole life ripped from your grasp."

"You did that to yourself," another voice said.

"Shut the fuck up," Williams roared. "You don't know anything."

"I know Lauren needed someone who was there for her. So did Ann and Linda. They didn't have that before they met me."

Franklin. Jesus, the guy had a death wish. Archer had little doubt Williams had a gun to the guy's head. The shred of doubt left when he heard the unmistakable cock of a trigger.

"I can be that man for them now. You won't be around much longer."

"Put it down, Williams," Dunn said firmly.

Williams snorted. "You think you're so smart, don't you? You've got this whole thing figured out. You're going to kill me and then what? Poor Lily goes boom. So does this place. Everything is set, and the only way to stop it is with me. Alive."

Archer faltered. Lily. He knew they needed to get her first. Instead, they were halfway across town and couldn't do a damn thing.

"You're lying."

Williams tsked. "All you guys are the same. Rodney thought I was lying, too. He never got a chance to find out just how serious I was about destroying the US government. This is just step one. Take out the infrastructure. We're so reliant on everything with a power button. TV, phones, computers, they all drag us away from what really matters. Once I take this away, people will start to lose faith in the government. The same way I did. I gave everything to this country, and all I got was a fucking divorce. I'm done playing by the rules. I'm going to take what I want—oof—"

Everything was silent for a minute. Archer touched his comms, checking that it was working, then gunshots echoed through the small room, setting him on high alert. He tensed, waiting for something. Shouting followed a door slamming, then the room emptied into the hallway in front of him.

"Where the hell did he go?" Dunn demanded.

"Who?"

"Williams. He went out a door in the back of the room. We can't get it open."

"A door?" Jenkins asked. "Where's Franklin?"

"He got hit. Dex is with him. Where does that door go?"

"I... I don't know. I didn't know there was another door there. I haven't been down here many times."

"Fuck."

"Door's open," Slade said through the comms. "Another hallway. It's empty."

"Fuck! He's gone."

"We have to get to Lily," Archer said.

"He could be heading there," Dunn agreed. "Let's get Franklin out of here. Mr. Jenkins, call an ambulance. We'll get him to the gate with you, then we need to go."

"Is this facility going to blow up?"

Jenkins hissed and shook his head. "No. You guys showed up before he finished uploading the virus. I can undo it."

"Mr. Franklin, was he at your house?"

He nodded. "Yes. With another guy. Blond, muscular.

Blake, I think he called him. And they had a woman in the basement."

"Where's your family?"

"Visiting her parents. They're not supposed to be home until next week."

"Good."

"We need to go," Archer growled. Blake. He couldn't believe Blake was involved in the whole thing. He knew there was something off about him. He should have trusted his instincts.

"Do you know where that hallway goes?" Dunn asked Franklin.

Franklin nodded. "Straight to the parking lot. He's long gone."

"Shit."

LILY SAT in the basement and prayed. She hadn't been overly religious, ever, but if there was ever a time she wanted to believe God was by her side, it was when she was moments from death.

A bang above her head had her screaming. Tears poured from her eyes. She waited for the rest of the explosion, the part that would kill her, but she swore she hear footsteps instead.

The door at the top of the stairs opened quietly. She stayed quiet. If Williams was back, she knew she couldn't say anything to stop him, so she didn't even need to try.

A sob ripped from her throat, and the door that was already closing swung back open.

"Lily?"

"Archer? Oh, my God. Archer? I'm down here."

Footsteps pounded down the stairs. When he came into view, he looked every bit the badass Jaymes always said his brother was. Decked out in so much tactical gear, Lily barely could tell it was Archer beneath it all.

He kneeled in front of her and quickly unlocked the handcuffs that held her ankles to the chair. She wanted to fall into his arms and forget everything that happened, but she had to warn him.

"Williams. He's the one who did all this. The guy who lives here, he's going to take the fall for it, but it was all Williams."

"We know," Archer said, cutting her off.

"Do you know he has this place rigged to blow up?"

Archer's face blanked carefully. "Stay here."

"What? Why? I want to get out of here."

"I need to make sure we can get you out safely. Lily, stay put." He pulled a gun out of a small pocket on his leg. "Take this. I'll be back for you as soon as I can be. If Blake or Williams come through that door, shoot them. Lock the door behind me."

She smiled. "The last time you told me to do that was for a very different reason."

Archer's hard features softened momentarily, then went rigid all over again. "Lock it, Lily."

She nodded and stuffed the emotion back down deep where it belonged.

Archer slid out the door, and she flipped the lock. Lily pressed her ear to the hollow wooden panel, trying to hear what was going on on the other side.

Silence.

Her hands shook uncontrollably. She couldn't get them to stop no matter what she did. It was stupid, but fear rolled through her, settling at the base of her spine and running up and down until she was practically choking on it.

Seconds passed like hours until she heard footsteps. Two knocks on the door.

Tentatively, Lily flipped the lock. Before she could open the door, someone on the outside pushed it in. The darkness masked his face, but she knew his body, his solidness.

Archer.

"Are you okay?" he asked, his large hands cupping her cheeks.

She couldn't see him, but when she shook her head, she knew his lips tugged down on the edges. He pulled her into his arms and kissed the top of her head.

"I'm sorry, honey. I'm so fucking sorry."

She clutched him, silently begging him never to leave her again. It hadn't been nearly long enough to fall in love with him, but the thought of losing him gutted her. She knew that meant she was in the danger zone.

And not just because there were people who wanted them both dead. Oh, no. Those guys were nothing compared to falling in love with a man who insisted he was unlovable, and incapable of loving someone else.

The bad guys could take her body, but Archer would destroy *her*.

24

———

Something wasn't right. Archer could feel it. Dex was going through the house with Dunn and Slade, but there was something off. Something that told Archer they were far from finished.

"We have to get out of here. Blake told me they were going to blow the house up. He said Williams has something—"

Archer held up a finger to her, telling her to wait.

"Williams could be here any minute. I've been here forever. Blake left. I don't know where he is. He said he had to wait but—"

"Lily," he hissed.

"Why are we staying here? The place is going to explode. They told me. There are bombs—"

"Shh," he growled at her.

"You never lis—"

The damn woman couldn't keep her trap shut if it killed her. The problem he was having was it might. He needed to hear what was going on. And she was making it impossible with her constant jabbering.

"I'm trying to listen," he hissed, nodding his head toward the door. Someone was out there. He'd bet his left nut.

"Someone's out there?" She whispered the same way she did everything else. At full fucking volume.

Archer was out of damn options. If she didn't shut up, he couldn't find out what was going on. And she clearly wasn't going to do it on her own.

He'd take one for the team. He knew how to keep a woman quiet.

He wrapped an arm around her waist and yanked her against him, plastering every inch of her curvy body to his. His lips came down on hers, sealing in whatever argument she was going to voice next. His tongue swept through, doing a thorough search of her, making sure he didn't leave a millimeter unexplored.

God, he fucking missed her. It had been just over twenty-four hours since she was in his arms and it was far too many, but she wasn't his. He knew he was kissing the one woman he couldn't have, the woman he'd never again have. It was wrong, and totally unfair to his brother, but Archer was enjoying the fuck out of it, out of her, while it lasted.

She whimpered, the soft sound reaching his ears and dragging him back to the moment. He didn't want to think about what they were doing. Why they were there. He just wanted to kiss her until she forgot any other man on the planet existed and decided she was his forever.

But forever wasn't going to happen. Not for him. Not with her or anyone else. He didn't deserve it after all his sins. Including kissing the fuck out of his brother's woman.

The slide of a shotgun had Archer pulling back half a second before the door exploded in front of them. He dove over the railing, taking Lily with him to the concrete basement floor below.

Archer spun, landing on his back with Lily on top of him. His body screamed from the pain, but all he could think of was keeping her safe.

A gun was in his hand before he could think, pointing straight at the door as someone broke through what was left of it. The slide snapped through the quiet again, and Archer trained his gun toward the sound.

The pop of his gun echoed in Archer's ringing ears seconds before the figure at the top slumped then rolled down the stairs. The shotgun landed a few feet away from the body, and Lily screamed.

"Blake. Oh, my God. That was Blake. You killed him."

Lily scrambled over to him, blood seeping onto the concrete floor beneath his still form. Archer forced himself up and over to the body. He kicked the shotgun away and stared down into the dead eyes of the man who tried to kill him.

Footsteps pounded toward them, racing down the stairs. They stopped when they saw Blake on the ground.

"The rest of the house is clear," Dunn said.

"I got all the explosives," Slade said. "He'd have taken out a city block. It's a good thing that wasn't his area of expertise. He was pretty fucking stupid how he set them up."

"Where's Williams?" Archer demanded.

Dunn shook his head. "In the wind. English is trying to track him, but he's gone as of now. He won't get away with this."

"Did Franklin stop everything at the plant?"

Dunn nodded. "Jenkins called. Said they're safe and Franklin's at the hospital now. He's okay."

Archer breathed a sigh of relief. "We need to call the cops."

"And border patrol," Slade added.

Dunn nodded and made the calls.

Lily sat on the floor next to Blake, crying. Archer watched her for a few seconds before he couldn't take it anymore. She was crying over a man who held her captive and threatened to kill her. And he was the one who put the bullets in the guy.

He was lucky he didn't put them in another one of his brothers. He didn't even pause to see who was there. He could have just as easily killed one of them instead of Blake.

Archer needed to get the fuck out of there.

Lily felt like she answered questions for hours. She probably did. The only reason they didn't insist on taking her to the police station was because Jaymes, Liam, and Adrian showed up, and Adrian insisted she get checked out at the hospital to make sure she was okay after being held captive for the better part of twenty-four hours. Her cheek was swollen and cut, but thankfully she didn't need stitches. She had a few bruised ribs, too. She was lucky.

Lily was released by the staff at the hospital with lots of well wishes and promises they'd visit her, and a week off to recover from her non-existent injuries. Archer told someone about jumping over the railing to the basement stairs so the ER staff insisted she take a few days to make sure she wasn't worse off than a little sore.

Archer saved her life. She didn't doubt that for a second. Even though Daniel told her Blake used non-lethal rubber rounds, she knew if she was shot with one of those, it would have hurt a hell of a lot more than just a scratch.

The fact that Archer even heard Blake coming

astounded her. She was so wrapped up in him that she forgot where they were and what was happening. He kissed her like she was still his.

Then he disappeared.

She hadn't seen him since he walked out of the basement and left her with a dead Blake and the others. Jaymes said Archer was getting checked out, too, but that was all he knew.

Lily walked outside with her arm around Jaymes's waist. He held her tight to his side, keeping her close to him and safe. She hated that her only thought was that she wished she was in Archer's arms instead of Jaymes's. It wasn't fair to him that she wanted his brother. Archer made his decision. And it wasn't her.

Dunn rode back to the apartment with them in Jaymes's truck. With Brady still on the loose, everyone was on high alert. Lily didn't think he'd try to do the same thing again, but he was crazy, and she had no idea what he would do.

"Are you okay?" Jaymes asked when they headed into the building.

Lily nodded, but she didn't feel it. She wasn't sure she'd ever be okay again after being held hostage by a crazy man and watching as someone she thought of as a potential friend was killed in front of her.

"Why don't you stay with me tonight?" Jaymes asked, his arm draped over her shoulders.

Lily shrugged. "Archer's probably going to stay with you. I'll let you two see each other. I'll be fine by myself."

"I'm not sure that's a good idea," Daniel interjected.

Lily shook her head. "I'm sorry, but I don't really want your opinion right now. I need a shower and some sleep. I'm starving, and I have a hard time believing Brady's going to grab me again. Plus, I learned my lesson last time."

"What lesson was that?" Jaymes asked.

Lily stopped at her door and smiled up at her best friend. "That your brother is the man you always told me he was. Cold, distant, and never one to say he's sorry. Whatever I thought we had was all in my imagination."

"Lily."

She shook her head and swallowed the tears welling. "Jaymes, don't. It's fine. I'll see you tomorrow sometime. Daniel, thank you and the others for saving us."

Daniel nodded and led Jaymes up the stairs to the third floor. Lily went into her apartment. The silence hit her first. After so many days with Archer and the rest of them around, the silence killed her. She turned on the TV for some noise, then ran a bath. Her apartment didn't have a soaker tub, but she was sore and would take what she could get.

She poured herself a very full glass of wine and carried it to the bathroom. The hot water felt good on her aches. She rinsed the cut on her cheek carefully, surprised at the amount of blood still there, then sat back. She sipped and cried and told herself she didn't need Archer anyway.

Lies. All of it.

ARCHER HESITATED at the door to Lily's apartment, but he didn't stop. He had nothing to say. He was heading out in the morning, back to DC, to the empty life he lived.

For once, Jack kept his mouth shut on their walk up the stairs. He didn't mention Lily once after Archer disappeared from the basement.

They walked into Jaymes's apartment to the sound of Dunn on the phone. The rest of the guys followed them in.

Jack and Dex immediately went to the fridge. Archer sat at the table with English.

"What's going on?" Archer nodded toward Dunn.

English glanced up, then turned his attention back to his screen. "Border patrol."

"Really?"

English shrugged. "That's what it sounded like."

"Shit."

"Pretty much."

Jack handed Archer a beer on his way to the living room. Archer leaned back in his chair and listened to Dunn's side of the conversation.

"Yes, sir. I understand. Okay. Seven, sir. Yes. Thank you, sir. Okay. Tomorrow. Thank you."

Dunn hung up the phone to a silent room. Everyone waited for him to say something, but he just stared at his phone.

"What kind of shit are we in?" Jack finally asked.

Dunn took his time looking up. "They want us to work on some special projects. They think Williams might still be in the area and since we know him the best, they want us to stay here."

"What?"

"You're kidding."

"Seriously?"

Dunn met the eyes of every man in the room and shook his head. "That's what the call was."

"How do they know who we are and what happened?"

"Jenkins called in the cops, and they called Homeland, and they called border patrol. I've never seen the government work this fast, but they want help. They found out about Blake and Williams getting Jaymes over the border and know they can't handle this on their own."

"Why us?" Slade asked.

"Williams," Dex said simply. "It makes sense. We know him. We almost caught him. He won't be able to catch us off guard again."

"Why do they think he's staying in the area?"

"Because this was personal," Dunn declared. "He came here because he was pissed about his wife leaving him. He wanted to put it all on her new husband. And his plan? That was to fuck with the country that he believes stole his family from him."

"Yeah, I heard it all," Archer grumbled.

Dunn faced him and shook his head. "No. You didn't. I turned off my comms. Williams killed Rodney. Not you. He set you up to take the fall because Rodney found out what he was going to do."

Archer's head spun, the image of his best friend's blank gaze fixed on his own. Archer went to a dark place when he realized he was the one who pulled the trigger. When Williams told him there was no one else in the area. He considered things no sane man should ever consider.

And it was all a fucking lie.

"Don't lie to me right now, Dunn."

Dunn shook his head and leveled Archer with a look so furious he took a step back. "I'm not lying. I'd never tell you that if it wasn't true. Yeah, I want to get that fucker, but him taking your brother and Lily was bad enough. I don't need to make shit up so you'll be willing to go after him. You don't need one more thing to blow up your fucking life."

Archer couldn't stop the flood of emotion welling up inside him. The pain. The guilt he carried for months. He withdrew from everyone because he knew, without a doubt, that he was damaged goods. That anyone who got close to him would end up hurt.

It wasn't true.

He blindly turned and left the apartment. His feet carried him down the stairs and outside. He needed the fresh air but being outside didn't help. He was suffocating.

He sunk to the grass near his SUV, knowing he couldn't drive, but desperate to get away. He dug his phone out of his pocket and called the one person who needed the news more than he did.

"Archer?" she said when she answered.

"Hi, Monica. We need to talk."

"I know. I've been trying to call you. Are you okay?"

He laughed mirthlessly. "No. Not even a little."

"I know none of this was easy. Losing him. He loved you."

Archer's throat filled with emotion and regret. He should have called Monica. She didn't even know the truth, and she was trying to console him.

"I didn't do it, Mon. I didn't kill him."

Her sharp intake of breath told him how much the thought of Rodney being gone still hurt her. It always would, for both of them. Losing family wasn't something you could walk away from without it leaving a permanent mark.

"I never thought you did, Archer."

"What do you mean?"

"You'd never hurt him. Even unintentionally. You loved him."

"I was angry at him."

She laughed. "So? That's what happens with brothers. Trust me, I have three of them. I know. It doesn't mean you wanted to hurt him."

"I shouldn't have been angry."

"Why were you?"

Archer shook his head. "I don't even remember."

"Then it wasn't that important. And it certainly wasn't something you would have killed him over."

"I didn't do it. I couldn't call you before, but I had to tell you."

"I'm guessing this means you know who did?" she asked, her voice hopeful.

Hope. Archer didn't know if he'd ever feel hopeful about anything again.

"Williams did."

She gasped. "No."

"I know you don't believe me, but—"

"No," she said, pain filling the distance between them, "I do. Rodney told me he thought Williams was doing something illegal. He was looking into it. He saw some emails or something. I told him to be careful."

"He knew. He found out the whole thing. That son of a bitch."

"Archer, what happened?"

Archer dropped his head into his hands and told her the whole story, from Lily's call that brought him to Niagara Falls to walking away from her in Franklin's basement and Williams getting away. When he was done, he couldn't believe it had only been a few days since it all started.

"You love her, don't you?" Monica asked quietly.

Archer scoffed. "I don't deserve love. Not with the things I've done in my life."

"Archer Ford, don't you dare say that. You are one of the best men I've ever met. Williams stole Rodney from me, but he gave Lily to you."

"No. I can't think that way. I can't think the only reason she's in my life is the same reason he isn't."

"Then think of it this way. Rodney knew you would need

someone. He knew you would need another person to lean on, someone to hold you up when you found out the truth. Someone to be there for you as you hunt for the man who killed my fiancé. Rodney brought her to you, and if you don't fix the mess you made with her, you'll be letting him down."

For the first time in days, maybe months, Archer could think about his best friend and laugh. Monica was right. Rodney would kick his ass if he knew he was walking away from the perfect woman because he was scared.

"She wants my brother."

Monica scoffed. "More excuses. Grow a set and tell her how you feel. You walked away from her, and from what you told me, she got taken because she thought she was going to see you. That doesn't sound like a woman who chose your brother to me. It sounds like a woman who knows who she really wants. And it isn't the brother who's been her best friend for years. It's the one who saved her and loved her and made her feel like she was special."

"She is, Mon. She is."

"Then go tell her, Archer. She needs to know."

Archer smiled. "You know, you sound like him."

Her answering grin was audible in her tone. "He had a tendency to rub off on everyone he knew."

"Yeah, he did. For the better."

25

LILY DRAGGED HERSELF OUT OF THE COLD TUB AND DRIED OFF. She wrapped herself in a fluffy robe and stuck her feet into pink flip flop slippers.

She opened the fridge and looked at the food she had no interest in eating. She snorted. Maybe she should get her heart broken more often. A wine only diet would do wonders for losing that fifty pounds she kept promising herself she'd get rid of one day.

She considered ignoring the glass and carrying the bottle to the couch with her, but she had a little bit of class left, so she emptied the bottle into her glass.

Why was it when she was depressed, everything on TV was about people falling in love? Best friends who became lovers. Enemies who decided they were in love. Even lovers who broke up then got back together because they couldn't be apart.

Where was a good horror flick when a lonely woman needed one?

She flipped over to Netflix and ignored the footsteps

racing up the stairs outside her door. More wine was definitely on the menu.

As soon as she read the descriptions, she knew she couldn't watch anything horror. It brought back the fear she felt just that morning being held captive and thinking she was going to die.

So, no romance.

No horror.

Definitely no action with badass alphas who saved the woman, then kissed her senseless like a guy was supposed to do.

Archer Ford ruined movies for her. The only thing left was slapstick comedy, and that annoyed her, or family movies. And God knew she didn't need anything to remind her she didn't, and never would, have a family.

She flipped off the TV, both with her finger and the remote, and tossed the remote aside. Maybe she should just finish her wine and go to sleep.

Lily was just about to climb into bed when someone knocked on her door. Her heart leapt into her throat. Blood roared in her ears. Terror had her paralyzed. Why did she think she could stay the night by herself? She was okay when everything was quiet, but someone was there for her.

She fumbled for her phone and sent Jaymes a text.

> Someone's outside my door. HELP!

> Who is it?

> I don't know.

> Did you look?

> Why are you asking me stupid questions? Send someone down here now! I'm so scared. Please, Jaymes. Don't let him take me again.

He didn't text back right away. Lily cowered in her bed, hiding under the covers. Maybe the guys would scare off whoever was there. Jack could sleep on her couch again. And she could just move in with Jaymes when everyone left. She didn't need her own apartment. Jaymes would make sure she was safe.

Her ears strained to hear something at her door, but the blood rushing through her head muffled everything else. She thought someone opened her door, and she started to cry. She wouldn't get away from him a second time. Where were the guys?

"Lily!" burst through the fear echoing inside her head. "Where are you?"

Archer? "Archer?"

"Where are you?"

"Archer! I'm in here. Oh, God. Did you get him?"

He stretched out on the bed next to her, pulling her tightly against his body. She buried herself in him, inhaling deeply so she could remember him. He was everything to her, but he wasn't hers.

She pushed away from him after a few minutes. "Was it Williams? Did you get him?"

Archer shook his head. "I'm sorry, honey. It wasn't Williams. It was just me knocking on your door. Why didn't you tell us you were so scared? Jaymes sent me a text saying you were inside freaking out that someone was here to get you."

"It was you?"

He nodded. "I wanted to talk to you."

Now she was pissed. "You had all day to talk to me. You walked away from me in that basement. You left me with a dead guy, a guy I kissed a couple days ago because I was mad at you, someone I could have been friends with. Dead from bullets you shot. And you just walked out."

Archer ran a hand through his hair. "I know. I shouldn't have walked out."

"You're damn right you shouldn't have."

They stared at each other across the room, her still in her fuzzy robe, under the covers of her bed, him staring down at her with more emotions than she could name racing through his eyes.

"I'm sorry. All my life, I've hurt the people I cared about. The people I loved. When I get mad, I lash out. And I was pissed off that they had the nerve to take you, and to use me to do it. When Blake came through that door, I shot. I didn't think twice about who was walking in, I just shot him. It could have been anyone."

"They wouldn't have shot through the door at us first," Lily argued.

Archer thought for a second, then laughed. "Yeah, I guess you're right. I didn't think about that."

She shook her head. "You did, you just didn't do it consciously. You're a soldier. You've spent years fighting to save the lives of your brothers and the people of this country. It's ingrained in you to protect people, not to hurt them."

"I've killed people, Lily. Most of them with my bare hands. That's why Jack called me Hulk. When I get angry, people get hurt or die."

Lily sucked in a breath and rose to her knees so she could look him in the eye more easily. "If you weren't willing to pull that trigger this morning, I'd be dead right now. Blake was going to kill me. Brady was, too."

"He killed Rodney."

Lily gasped. "No."

Archer nodded and ran a hand down his neck. "He told Dunn. Rodney knew something was going on, and Williams took him out. I talked to his fiancée, and she said Rodney was looking into Williams. That's why she asked me to bring him home. She knew it was going to get bad if he actually found anything."

"Obviously, he found something."

Archer nodded once. "Yeah. And he paid for it. Williams killed a man he trained, a man he called his brother. He'll stop at nothing to finish what he started here."

Lily closed her eyes and fought back the tears. She'd never sleep again, no matter how much wine she drank, knowing Williams could come back for her.

"I'm scared," she admitted.

He smiled. "Me, too. But I'm not going to let him take you from me again."

She drew in a ragged breath. "What are you talking about?"

"I'm not leaving you again, Lily. Not if you want me like I want you."

"What?" she breathed. It had to be the wine. It was making her hear things. Things that couldn't possibly be true.

He moved toward her, his hand reaching out for hers. She watched as it moved closer and closer, knowing she was far more drunk than she thought. Then his hand connected with hers, and that spark she always felt when he touched her ran up her arm.

"Dunn got a call from the border patrol. They want us to stick around here and help them find Williams. The rest of the team wants to stay."

"What?" she asked again. Nothing he said was making any sense.

"Are you okay?" he asked.

She shook her head. "I must have had too much to drink. I thought you said you're staying and you want me. You're going to have to start from the beginning."

He laughed, a short burst that speared through her. She loved his laugh. Almost as much as she loved the way he grunted and moaned when he filled her. And the dirty things he whispered in her ear before he came inside her. And the way he protected her. How he held her close after they made love. The feel of his fingers caressing her skin when he thought she was sleeping. Everything about him.

She was never going to get over him. And that sucked.

"Lily, I need you to listen to me. Can you hear me, honey?"

She nodded.

"Everything you heard is true. I'm staying. I want you. Not just for tonight, but for every night for the rest of my life. I'm not going to leave you alone again, sweetheart. You're going to be right here with me forever. If you'll take a broken, bruised, and angry SEAL who doesn't deserve a second chance."

Her heart swelled as quickly as her eyes overflowed with tears. All she could do was nod and wave him closer. He chuckled as she buried her face in his neck and cried. He was hers. And he wasn't going anywhere.

ARCHER SPENT the next week settling into life with Lily. They had their issues, like who washed whose back first when they got in the shower, and who got to come first every night, but they worked it all out.

He took her with him to DC to collect the few things he had there that he cared about. Most of his stuff went to the local veterans organization to help others who needed furniture and accessories. Archer made a sizable donation in Rodney's name while he was there, too.

His favorite time of day was early in the morning. They both got up early, earlier than either of them liked, but he was quickly becoming a fan of putting his morning wood to good use inside the woman he loved.

After he made her scream a few times, and cleaned the dirty, dirty woman he loved in the shower, he pulled on a pair of shorts and followed her to the kitchen.

"What do you want for breakfast today?"

He shrugged. "Brain food. I need to find Williams."

"Do you think he's still in the area?"

Archer sighed and nodded. "Yeah. Dunn has Franklin and his family under surveillance, but I think he's biding his time."

"I still can't believe he had us all believing he was one of the good guys."

Archer grimaced. He felt even more duped. He turned to Williams after Rodney died. He trusted the guy. Williams told him death was a part of war and that not everyone will go home. The asshole tried to make him feel better about murdering someone knowing the whole time that Archer didn't do it. Williams set him up to take the fall.

Dunn notified the SEALs about Williams. They needed to be aware of the shit storm coming. If Williams blamed the SEALs for his wife leaving, Dunn and Dex were convinced he'd try to get back at the military also. No one really knew what he was capable of.

"There are always going to be bad guys disguised as good guys. I'm just sorry you got dragged into all this."

Lily shook her head. "I'm not. It brought you to me. And it showed me I can handle things I never thought I'd be able to do. Not that I want a repeat, but I handled it."

Archer pulled her against him and kissed her lips. "You did."

They got lost in their kiss until a loud knock on the door broke them apart. Lily jumped at the noise.

"Are you okay?"

She nodded, but there was fear in her eyes. She was strong, though. Lily wouldn't run and hide with him by her side. And he promised he always would be.

Archer opened the door for Jaymes and the rest of the team. Archer mended the fences with his brother and found himself spending more and more time with him. For the first time ever, he was wishing he'd gotten to know Jaymes better, but he finally had the opportunity.

"You guys have breakfast? I'm out of food. These massive idiots have eaten everything I own in two days," Jaymes complained.

Lily laughed and nodded, welcoming them all in. She headed to the kitchen with Jaymes while the others went to the living room. Jack hung back and talked to Archer.

"How are things going with you two?"

Archer grinned, checking out Lily's curvy ass. He couldn't wait to get his hands on it again. "Perfect. She's amazing. I got lucky."

Jack snorted. "Damn right you did. If she met me first, you'd have been out of luck."

"Sorry, Jack, but I don't think so," Lily said, interrupting them for a kiss.

Archer took full advantage of the moment and swept his

tongue through her mouth, plunging in repeatedly until she moaned. He grew hard against her soft stomach, aching to repeat their morning workout. Sex with a beautiful woman beat PT every day.

"Get a room!" Dunn shouted from the other room.

Archer finally let her up, keeping her close as he yelled back, "We have our own place. You invaded us, so you're going to need to get over it."

"Yeah, yeah. We have important business to discuss. Where are we going to look for Williams?"

Archer shook his head. "You sure know how to kill a good boner, Pres."

"We have work to do," Dunn growled.

"Who pissed in his Cheerios?" Archer asked Jack.

Jack shrugged. "He's been like this for days. He was Williams' second, and he didn't see this coming. Apologized to Jaymes yesterday. He thinks the whole thing is his fault."

Lily wrapped her arms around Archer's waist. "It's Brady's fault. He's the one who made the choices he made. He was good at hiding who he really was."

Jack nodded. "Yeah, but Dunn can't shake that he should have known. He feels like he failed somehow."

"He needs to get laid. That made me feel better when I blamed myself for Jaymes."

Archer tickled her side, and she squealed. "Is that all I am to you? Someone to take your frustrations away?"

She smiled. "Of course not. But you're a lot better at it than baking ever was. And I might lose weight after all the cardio we're doing. Cupcakes go straight to my ass."

Archer palmed her ass and squeezed. "It's a perfect ass."

Lily grinned up at him. "What are you guys going to call your team?"

"Call ourselves?" Jack asked. "Why do we need to call ourselves something?"

Lily scoffed like it was the dumbest question she'd ever heard. "Every great team has a name. You need one."

"We don't need a name."

"Yeah, you do," Jaymes argued. "She's totally right."

"Why?" Archer asked.

Jaymes and Lily both ignored him and turned to each other. "Brotherhood?"

"Badass."

"Nice," she said. "Fabulous Brotherhood of Badasses."

"Fabulous Brotherhood of Military Badasses," Jaymes said.

They both started laughing.

"You two are crazy," Archer said. He still thought his brother had a thing for Lily, but she'd made it clear she was only interested in one Ford brother. Archer got over his jealousy and set to learning everything there was to know about her. His current favorite was her ever present sense of humor.

"Ooh, I know," Lily said. "Foreign Borders Overseen by Military Badasses."

Jaymes nodded. "I like that."

Even Jack agreed. He whistled to get the attention of the room. "Lily has a name for our team."

Lily grinned at him. "You guys should be Foreign Borders Overseen by Military Badasses."

The guys exchanged a look. "What?" Dunn asked.

"I like it," English said without looking up from his computer.

"Me, too."

"Even better," Lily said, "you'd be F-BOMB."

There was no arguing with her after that. They were definitely F-BOMB.

JAYMES WATCHED Lily from across the room as she laughed at something Archer said. His lips curled up in response without conscious thought. She always had a way of making him feel like everything was going to be okay. From the moment they met, he knew she was special. She never saw it in herself, but he did. It was why he fell in love with her in the first place.

He always told himself one day he'd admit his feelings to her, but now it was too late. She was in love with his brother and Jaymes was forgotten. The friend who helped them get together. Not that he did anything besides being too weak to defend himself, protect himself.

Lily was the one thing that kept him from completely losing his mind when he was in that basement. Her face and the hope that he would see her again forced him to survive. He promised himself when he got out, he'd stop dragging his feet and tell her how he felt.

Until he saw her and realized she'd fallen for his brother. Jaymes was in a hole for almost two weeks, not sure he'd ever see daylight or the woman he loved again, and she was starting a life with his brother.

It stung more than it should. Lily was never his. She was his best friend, but that was where their relationship stopped. He wanted more, but she never gave him any indication she felt the same way, and he always hid his feelings. Jaymes wondered...

No, he wasn't going to do that to himself. Or Lily or

Archer. They were together, and Jaymes was alone. As always.

Jaymes smiled when she laughed a second time and wondered if he'd ever feel like himself around her again. He wanted to let go of how he felt about her, but it wasn't something he could flip a switch and be done with. Especially after his feelings for her were his one and only focus outside of dying for weeks.

Archer kissed the side of Lily's head and met Jaymes's gaze. It wasn't threatening or menacing. It was just curious. Jaymes was fairly sure his brother had no idea how he felt about Lily, but even if he knew, Jaymes couldn't blame Archer for loving her. Lily was the kind of woman who was impossible not to love.

Archer made a move to approach Jaymes, but Jack reached his side first. "You doing okay?"

"I'm not sure it's possible for me to be okay yet."

Jack nodded. "Totally understand that. I'd be the same. I've been the same."

"You seem pretty fearless," Jaymes told the SEAL honestly. It was hard to imagine any of them not on top of their game.

"I know how to hide it, but I also know how to manage it. Managing it is better than hiding it."

"Right now, hiding feels like the only option."

"Want to go for a run in the morning?"

"Why?"

Jack shrugged. "Because I like to run. I never got out of the habit. You know your way around. I figured if you go with me I can learn some new routes."

"Is that how you're going to play this?" Jaymes asked. It was a thinly veiled attempt to make it seem like Jack wasn't taking pity on Jaymes and trying to help him.

"Play what? I might try to find an apartment around here. If I do, it'll be good to know some of the paths and roads."

"And you can't do that alone?"

"Nope. Be ready at six."

Jack walked away, leaving Jaymes to shake his head. Leaving the apartment, being out in the open, wasn't something he was ready for yet, but hiding wasn't going to be an option forever. At some point, he needed to manage his fear. And running might be a step in that direction.

Lily laughed at something Archer said and captured Jaymes's attention again. It would have been easy to hate her for choosing his brother, but Jaymes couldn't. Just like he couldn't blame Archer for loving her, he couldn't blame her for loving him. Archer was always the alpha. Everyone wanted him in their life, in their world. Including Jaymes.

Accepting Archer and Lily's relationship was one thing, but building a new one between the brothers was another. Jaymes didn't know his brother anymore. It had been years since they'd spent time together. The only reason Archer was still there was because of Lily, not because of Jaymes. But Jaymes didn't get a vote in Archer's life. He wouldn't steal their happiness or wish for it to end. It was like handling his fear. He had to find a way to manage his feelings around it.

Too bad he couldn't outrun them.

THANK **you** so much for reading Archer and Lily's story! I hope you enjoyed getting to know them and the rest of F-BOMB! F-BOMB: SEALs Love Curves continues with Jaymes' story. He's been forgotten by the woman who was there for him forever, but someone new needs his help. One look at the curvy beauty on his mother's doorstep with fear in her eyes tells Jaymes he has to help. Not that it's a hardship. Kelsea is beautiful, smart, and funny. He can't resist. Get Forgotten now!

IF YOU CAN'T GET ENOUGH of Archer and Lily, you can read more from them! Their story isn't quite over. Archer has faced death many times over, but nothing scares him as much as looking for the perfect ring for Lily. Especially when he finds out danger is still out there. Fiancée is only available to newsletter subscribers. Sign up today to get your free copy.

WANT to fall for her brother's best friend? Andie never thought of Cody as anyone other than her brother's best friend. But Cody has been in love with her for years. When he starts remodeling her house, the two of them develop a connection neither of them expected. One that could lead to Love At First Fight. Start reading now!

ABOUT THE AUTHOR

USA TODAY Bestselling Author Mary E Thompson spent most of her childhood wishing she had a few less curves. She hid in the pages of books because her favorite characters never cared what size her clothes were. Now, neither does Mary, and she writes stories that celebrate women like her. Real women who have curves, chase dreams, and find love, because we should all be happy, no matter our dress size.

Mary spends her non-writing time with her husband and two kids, watching too much TV, cheering for her hometown football team (Go Bills!), and hiding chocolate from her family.

Visit https://MaryEThompson.com/ to sign up for Mary's newsletter, **Romancing the Curves**. Subscribers get free ebooks and other fun stuff, like exclusive, members only content and giveaways, plus are the first to know about new releases and sales!